THE VICTOR PART II

Andrew Meade

ANDREW MEADE

Copyright © 2014 Andrew Meade

All rights reserved.

ISBN-13:978-1492118619

CONTENTS

Prologue	6
Chapter One	13
Chapter Two	27
Chapter Three	36
Chapter Four	51
Chapter Five	64
Chapter Six	81
Chapter Seven	89
Chapter Eight	98
Chapter Nine	116
Chapter Ten	129
Chapter Eleven	140
Chapter Twelve	151
Chapter Thirteen	158
Chapter Fourteen	182
Chapter Fifteen	201
Chapter Sixteen	214
Chapter Seventeen	234

THE VICTOR PART II

PROLOGUE

Semerkhet strode briskly down the corridor, his face contorted in rage. As he drew near the archway leading to the rear of the courtyard in which his gladiators trained, he expected to hear the commotion there that he had grown so accustomed to. Instead he heard a loud, clear voice addressing all those present.

As Semerkhet stepped through the threshold of the arch, his sharp, darting eyes quickly examined the expansive area. The training equipment was deserted, and all the fighters were gathered around the young man who spoke. His compelling words drew the attention of anyone who listened. And with the first word Semerkhet heard spoken, he knew what this scum was. "*Jesus,*" the boy said. A Christian. Semerkhet cursed under his breath.

Just then Diomed, one of Semerkhet's most highly honored servants and head of gladiatorial training, trotted purposefully into the courtyard. He assessed the situation in a flash and waded into the crowd around the Christian. Semerkhet saw his head bobbing a few inches above the others as the tall man walked on. He emerged a few seconds later from the ring and was standing a few feet away from the boy. The young man prepared to run, but

Diomed snatched a firm grip on his shoulders and forced him onto his knees, waiting for him to fall into submission. When any struggle left the boy, he heaved him back up and journeyed back through the crowd to deliver the perplexing youth to Semerkhet.

Semerkhet waited expectantly until the Christian was flung onto the hard packed earth in front of him. "Bring me a sword," commanded Semerkhet without lifting his gaze from the defiantly confident boy now slowly rising to his feet. A few seconds later, the hilt of a sword was pressed into Semerkhet's hand. He wrapped his long knobby fingers around the leather grip, and when Diomed let the perfectly balanced weight of the refined weapon fall into his master's hand, the lanista recognized it as a scimitar.

Semerkhet's cold stare never wavered, nor did the powerful gaze of the Christian. "You should know," said Semerkhet silkily, "that the following of that wretched cult is not allowed in my ludus."

"Do what you will to me," said the Christian in an ever so slightly wavering voice, "but never shall I stop praising my Savior."

"Save me that putrid speech at least," Semerkhet said.

"I love my Lord more than life."

"Fool," scoffed Semerkhet. He struck out with the scimitar. The dead body collapsed nearly instantly and Semerkhet, prepared for another blow, stayed his hand. He was splattered with gore and puffed air heavily out of his nostrils. He tilted back his head and roared into the open sky in rage.

Everyone stepped away, fearful of their maddened lanista. Then, a deep rumble rippled across the sky as Semerkhet still faced it. It drew everyone's attention upward, where dark, ominous storm clouds were condensing, churning and writhing as swift flashes of lightning streaked across their gray surfaces every few seconds.

Abruptly, a bolt of lightning leapt out from the mass of clouds like a fiery sword and exploded into the ground before Semerkhet. The old man's body was flung into the air, and he landed again an instant later with a sickening thud. Everyone stared at the crumpled, prone body in shock. His skin was scorched, his bones crushed. He was most certainly dead.

Diomed lay on his straw pallet late that night, dumbfounded by the death of his master. He was startled particularly at the familiarity of the event. Lightning striking out from the heavens to decimate the enemies of Christians. This thought immediately sent him to that of the boy who had escaped the ludus a few months ago. News had spread quickly of the escaped slave who had prayed to the god of the Jews, receiving an answer in the form of lightning busting through a tavern's roof to protect him. Bacchus, the man he and Semerkhet had sent to chase Adir, had failed and never returned. Diomed guessed he was dead. He knew that it was him who had been the target of the fire from the sky in Araby. Diomed had so many questions, and somehow he knew without a doubt that only Adir could ever answer them. He wanted, or needed desperately, to speak with Adir.

Just then, Diomed's attention was drawn to a flicker in the corner of his private quarters. He sat up suddenly in alarm as he saw the unearthly light expand to several feet across. A humanoid figure suddenly stood there where there had been no-one before. But this figure was definitely not a man. He was in gut wrenching astonishment at his presence as he faced the stranger. The glow that seemed to spark from his skin lit the room. The man's face was of a golden radiance, like a ray of the sun. His steely eyes shone like a hot flame. He was clothed in a flowing silk tunic, and a belt heavily adorned with jewels and wrought of what looked like platinum wrapped around his waist. His limbs were like polished bronze, and held high in his right hand was the most amazing feature of all. A mighty, majestic sword was there. It seemed to radiate power beyond imagining. Pure white flames caressed the flawless blade. Diomed cowered in fear.

"Who are you?" he asked timidly.

"An angel of the Lord," the stranger replied. Diomed trembled. The voice of the angel, even in a simply spoken word, was like a hundred men speaking in perfect unison, with the feeling and sincerity of one man.

"Why are you here?" Diomed further questioned.

"The Lord has chosen you. You will follow the will of Christ, your savior, who sits enthroned at the Creator's right hand. The Spirit of God will guide you all of your days, Diomed."

Diomed was bewildered. What would the Lord have him do, and how did the angel even know his name?

The angel looked into his eyes and spoke as if he knew his thoughts. "The God of the Universe knows your name, and everything about you. You are His beloved creation, and now He commands you to leave this place of vanity and join Adir, declaring the Good News of Christ."

With that, the angel vanished. There was no sight or sound that announced his departure in the slightest. He was simply gone in an instant. Diomed needed no more urging than the abrupt words spoken by the angel. He hurried from his pallet and busied himself preparing a pack for his journey. The whole thing weighed more than a dozen pounds when he slung it onto his back, but it would be enough for the trip, as far as he knew. Lastly, he fastened to the pack Adir's falcata, a sword thin at the base of the blade and filling out into a wide blade for hacking before tapering to a point. The sword, from Adir's days of training and fighting as a gladiator, was not for his own use, as he had already packed his own gladius. He was quite certainly going to need it on his journey.

Adir's father had once wielded the same sword, he remembered. When he and his child-bearing wife had been attacked by bandits, he fought valiantly. But at last he had been killed, and all his possessions, along with his wife had fallen into the bandit's hands. Adir was born soon after, and when he was about three, his mother died and he was sold into another master's slavery the same year, for a cheap price. For eight years, Adir was in the desert, traded from one Bedouin nomad to the other, until Semerkhet finally bought him, and the sword, which had been traded with him since their capture by the bandits.

Diomed deserted his reminiscence and exited his small room. The corridors of the villa were lit by torches in brackets lining the masonry walls in intervals of a hundred feet or so. Between the oases of dancing orange light, Diomed surreptitiously crept through the pitch blackness. He knew the villa well enough to navigate it with ease even in the dark of night. A few minutes later, Diomed was emerging from the shadow of one of the massive pillars that ringed the villa. He was now hastening across the hilly grounds that were directly outside the entrance to the estate. Just inside the gate to Semerkhet's property were a beautiful orchard and a vineyard.

Nestled inside a grove of trees, whose leaves were just beginning to plunge into the brilliant hues of autumn, was Semerkhet's grave. At the head of the mound of freshly upturned soil was a large granite headstone fitted with a sprawling epitaph. Diomed was surprised by the sense of melancholy that settled over him. For as long as he could remember, this was the only life he knew. And in less than a day it had all changed. Now he would be leaving it forever. He left the grave with a hushed gasp of unwithdrawn trepidation.

CHAPTER ONE

Primus Imperious Titus was a hardened legionnaire, though he was only sixteen. His strong figure was garbed for war. Glistening armor adorned his body; a helmet was fastened to his head, over the short-cropped blonde hair. A gladius within his scabbard hung to the right from his waist. A red tower shield to his left leaned against the railing of the galley ship on which he stood. It swayed placently in the shallow water. Around him the eighty-six other men in his century muttered their shared hatred of sailing.

Their speech was quieted when the imposingly statured officer at the fore of the galley ship turned to address them. A scarlet plume sprouted from his helmet and his gladius hung at his left side, marking him as an officer. He was not the centurion, or the leader of the century, but rather the second-in-command, or optio. He was assuming the role of his superior, centurion Maximus Quintus, a decorated war hero who was elsewhere performing a special mission for the Emperor himself.

Valerius and his century, along with all of the centuries that together formed the first cohort of a powerful Roman legion, were poised to wipeout the last rebels resisting the conquest of the first son of the late Vespasian, Titus' namesake. The First Cohort advanced steadily on the shoreline of Judea even as the other cohorts of the legion were plunging into the fray of battle themselves. As the line of galley ships approached the shore, milling with Jewish rebels readying themselves for a battle, three artillery ships only a hundred yards from land readied ballistae and catapults.

The galley ships crept across the turquoise water painfully slowly. "Ready!" Valerius shouted in a commanding, regal tone. Titus slipped his arm into the leather straps on the interior of the tower shield and pulled it away from the railing, revealing Titus' javelin where it also rested against the rough wood. He clutched it around the shaft and positioned it at his side. He stiffened his body to an attentive position and attempted to clear his thoughts of the anxiety that always preceded a cataclysmic battle. He focused his mind instead on the primitive concept of the fighting ahead.

The Romans were jarred as the vessel was cast up onto the sandy shore by the surging waves. The onslaught began. The huge black masses of the catapults' fodder would loom high in the afternoon sky for a few brief moments before plunging back to Earth to wreak havoc on the ranks of the Jewish rebels. They tossed up huge volleys of sand and flung prone bodies aside, while the ones coated in pitch and set ablaze provided striking spectacles as they soared to their targets where they emblazoned the horizon with the immense fireballs. Titus heard the faint hiss of the ballistae bolts before they disappeared into the Jewish army.

Agonized cries assaulted Titus' ears, though he could scarcely consider the travesties unfolding around him as his century was ordered off the ship. Dark streaks whisked about Titus, and the legionnaire subconsciously recognized them as the Jews' arrows. A pebble, evidently launched from the sling of a Jew, ricocheted off Titus' helmet, leaving a considerable dent. Titus raised his tower shield to ward off the projectiles as he shuffled forward with the rest of his century to the fore of the sea craft. Titus, with Valerius and the others in the first rank of their century, unhesitantly dropped off the galley ship, Titus' feet leaving shallow depressions in the sand as he landed lightly.

The legionnaires moved forward as their comrades descended to the shore where they clambered to hastily form a defensive position, all the while buffeted by the projectiles of the rebels. They managed to form a tortoise position, where the shields were held to from a barrier around the whole of the century, even as the first wave of Jews lurched away from the sea of their comrades to charge the advancing Romans. In unison, the Romans hurled their javelins into the tangle of limbs. Many Jews collapsed and many more were impaled by their fallen colleagues. The legionnaires exploited the brief and slight lapse in assault to draw their gladiuses and prepare for the melee to come. As Titus clenched his fist around the ivory handle, he pondered the fact that Romans considered themselves above their savage foes for their advanced weaponry. Titus was briefly disdainful of the Empire's arrogant nature, as he knew that any fighting, no matter how technologically advanced, was barbarism, but this notion was eclipsed by his ever present awe of the Empire's supremacy and overwhelming accomplishments.

The Judeans fell upon them, raining down blows with swords and spears. The dozens upon dozens of blades sped through the air around Titus, narrowly missing him. As the throng of enemies swelled around Titus, he drew back his arm and then thrust his sword into the mass of bodies. He felt substantial contact and saw a body collapse in the mayhem. The familiar pang of guilt struck him in the chest and for a moment he could not draw breath. He pulled his arm back behind his shield, and as he did so, a tanned fist curled around the hilt of a scimitar struck him in the face, knocking him back and opening a gap in the shields for the Jew to leap through before being cut down by Valerius a moment later. The optio was a fierce warrior, though not as much so as Quintus, and the ranks of the Jews shattered when they met him, like high tide on a boulder jutting from shore.

Seeing the partially successful infiltration on the part of their comrade, the other Jews were keen to follow suit, surging upon the tower shields with renewed ferocity. Titus threw his weight into his shield and rammed the silver boss into the face of one of the rebels, who slunk back clutching at his face. Titus soon received a cut on his forearm, which smarted severely, and he retaliated by hacking haphazardly at the Jews. An arrow flew past Titus' head, and he soon sensed someone collapse behind him, followed by the movement of another man taking his place.

The century battled on and Titus was violently jarred again and again by the zealous attempts of the rebels to break the formation. The blade of Titus' gladius turned scarlet as he repeatedly plunged it into the crowd in front of him. With colossal effort, the tortoise formation crept along the desert sands, ever so slowly but efficiently crushing the fords of the Jews. Stones and arrows drummed against the tower shields raised over the heads of the legionnaires. Titus knew not how long they battled, for any trivial thoughts were expelled from his mind, leaving only sporadic flashes of reflex, both learned and inborn. Finally, Titus' century reached the area devastated by the artillery. Fiery wreckage of the catapults' damage was scattered around over the blackened sand among the strewn bodies. The Romans were halted in the progress as they were reluctant to break ranks. Rather than attack the vulnerable Romans, the Jews fled. They disappeared over a sand dune and Titus heard Valerius roar in outrage beside him.

"This is our chance to crush the Jews!" he shouted. "AFTER THEM!" Even as he bellowed, Valerius abandoned the formation to charge after the Jews. His century imitated him, screaming and bolting forward, Titus among them. The other centuries, now arriving at this point, followed suit as well.

Soon the hundreds of Romans were charging down the far side of the dune, to be met with a rain of arrows and stones like nothing Titus had ever seen. Titus stopped abruptly, spraying sand, and crouched behind his shield. Two arrows were buried in the wood and a stone glanced off of the rim. Scores more were not so quick as to seek cover behind their shields and collapsed dead or dying where they stood, their prone bodies heaping upon each other. Titus tried not to retch as his insides churned.

The shower of projectiles ceased as suddenly as it had begun. When the remaining Romans recovered, the Jews were running again, dropping their weapons as they went. Titus stared dumbfounded at the swords, spears, bows and slings left by their enemies. The Romans, by unspoken consent, pursued them once more, and after navigating the shifting dunes for several minutes, they saw the defensible structure to which the Jews had fled. It was a vast stone building, stretching across the unruly sands of the desert, breaking the monotony of the terrain with its majesty and splendor. The hundreds of Jews were gathered on an immense stone porch, surrounded on three sides by stairs also crowded with Jews, and on the fourth side was a bare wall, permeated solely by oak double-doors, to which the Jews seemed to be struggling. Huge pillars on the porch supported an awning that cast the whole affair in its shadows.

Titus glanced to his right and saw Valerius grinning maniacally. "NOW THE SWINE WILL BE SLAUGHTERED!" he roared, and with that sprinted down to the crowd. Titus wheeled around to face the standard-bearer, adorned in animal skins and holding high a metal eagle, the symbol of Rome. Titus knew him as his good friend and comrade, Herax.

"We can't attack them, they're unarmed!" declared Titus indignantly.

ANDREW MEADE

"Then they're stupid," retaliated Herax before following in the footsteps of their optio. Titus reluctantly gave chase anew.

The Romans poured into the fray of the crowd, in no formation, hacking haphazardly at any Jew they could reach. The sight of dozens of mutilated bodies falling dead before his fellows gravely dismayed Titus. The Romans were separated and disordered, and the Jews were desperately fighting for their lives with their bare hands, overwhelming the Romans. Titus was disappearing under the sea of thrashing limbs, barraged with their blows to him. His body ached and his vision blurred like a veil descending over his eyes.

Suddenly, the Jews scattered, deserting Titus and trying with renewed vigor to enter the building. Titus remained where he was, sprawled on the bloodstained surface of the stone porch where he had apparently collapsed during the tumult. He hastily came back to his feet and found the remaining Romans scrambling to form organized ranks, but rather than facing the Jews who now opened the oak doors and were pouring into the building, they faced a new army, much larger, beating down upon them from the desert. There were few projectiles, for the majority of this new army carried swords or spears. The dozens of bodies strewn across the porch hindered the

Romans as they tried to defend themselves, and they had no upper hand.

The battle raged with ferocity that astonished Titus as the opposing army crushed the Romans with steady progress. After minutes of brutal fighting that seemed more like hours, alarm seemed to ripple like a wave through the crowd. Titus had just disengaged from an enemy, and now cast a glance to the sky. A spherical inferno was descending upon them. For a moment, Titus was confused as well as terrified until he heard a cry of outrage behind him, "The catapults weren't supposed to launch now!" Realization struck Titus and he knew at once what he had to do.

He wheeled round and ran for the open doorway. He was jostled as many other Romans did the same. They poured into the corridors of the building. Titus managed to stay standing, but many more were trampled. The fiery boulder crashed into one of the pillars, and they both shattered. The flame spread in waves, tearing through the crowd. The stone overhang collapsed, and the gargantuan fireball blasted the walls into hundreds of rocks raining through the air and blew the huge oak doors into splinters. The limp bodies of the dead were flying in all directions. Debris, fire and dust, along with the bodies of Romans and their enemies alike bowled over the Romans in the corridor of the building.

Titus was bombarded by debris, and he was soon thrown to the ground by a particularly large length of wood. His consciousness began to wane, but he still clung to his waking thoughts. Finally, he began to come to and he forced himself into a sitting position. More than a thousand men had been fighting there before the pitch-coated boulder had struck. The enormous quantities of rubble hid only a fraction of the countless bodies that now littered the corridor, porch and surrounding area. Titus removed his arm from the leather straps of his ruined shield and discarded it. His helmet had been knocked askew and was so mangled it was more of a nuisance than anything else. He pulled it off his head and tossed it aside. His body was blackened by the fireball, his skin torn in many places. His armor was blackened and mangled as well, though still effective, Titus supposed. Titus' body was marred with so many wounds he could not identify the pain radiating from any one of them. It rather melted together there and washed over him with the ebb and flow of a rippling pond. Titus located his gladius lying amidst the debris and he snatched it up by its ivory handle. He now noticed that a few more men were stirring.

Valerius was standing, his fingers fumbling with the chin strap on his plumed helmet. When it was secure, he fetched his gladius from the floor. "Anyone who can fight, come with me!" Valerius shouted. The movement in the corridor increased, and soon fifty people stood, many near collapsing, all battered and scathed. "We're going to finish off those Jews."

"We can't!" exclaimed another man. "There are hardly fifty men here! Only a score of them are able to fight, and you want us to destroy the Jews that the whole cohort couldn't defeat?"

"A score is enough," replied Valerius. "This is what Quintus would do, and as officer in his stead, I will defend his honor and the honor of Rome." Titus remembered the slaughter of the unarmed Jews and his mind was made up at once. He would never again participate in such bloodshed. He rotated the gladius in his hand so that the point faced the ground and strode forward to Valerius. He thrust out his arm, gesturing for Valerius to take the handle.

"I hereby resign from the legion of Rome." Valerius wrapped his strong fingers around Titus' forearm and flung aside his arm. "YOU CANNOT RESIGN!" Valerius roared. "You, as everyone else here, are bound to twenty-five years of service under the eagle. You have only completed one. You will follow me. NOW!"

Valerius rounded on his heels and charged down the corridor. Any Roman who could still fight staggered after him. Titus spotted Herax, who still clutched the Roman standard in his left hand, a gladius in the other. Titus reluctantly followed the twenty-strong entourage. They soon reached an intersection of the corridors, and Valerius hesitated briefly as he could not determine whether to go right or left. Valerius lowered his gaze and examined the floor, where he spotted traces of blood. Without a word he set off to follow it, as did the others. They followed the blood in the same fashion for several minutes until they slowed by unspoken consent. They could hear noises, albeit quiet, other than their pounding footsteps. Titus began to hear snatches of discernible words, and was shocked.

"They're praying!" he declared.

"Fools," muttered Valerius and bounded off to face the Jews.

The Romans soon burst into a large room crowded with almost a hundred Jews. On the other side were open terraces, and in the back of the room stood a robed man whose hands were raised to the sky as he spoke passionately. In front of him were three bowls of burning incense on stands. "This is a temple," said Titus suddenly. This did nothing to faze Valerius, who waded into the midst of kneeling Jews, hacking in every direction.

Soon, gore was showering all the Romans save Titus, as the Jews fell before them like wheat on a harvest day. Titus remained standing in the threshold of the doors trying to avert his eyes from the slaughter. Then he spotted a girl crouching a few feet from the massacre, yet she seemed unaffected by it. Her head was bowed, and she was praying fervently. Titus stepped forward and began to walk slowly toward her. She suddenly looked up at him and reeled away in alarm. Titus had no intention of hurting her, for there was something about her that intrigued him. He tossed aside his gladius and she looked relieved.

He was soon standing before her.

"Who are you?" he asked.

"A follower of the Christos," she replied. Titus immediately recognized the Latin term for Christ. "I came here to worship in the land God gave to His chosen people."

Titus felt a heel against his side and was roughly pushed away by the powerful kick. Valerius was now standing in front of the girl, drenched in gore, his sword poised above his head to kill her. "Jews are rebellious to the grave," Valerius said, "So that's where they must go." Suddenly, the ground trembled and then violently jerked. Everyone was knocked to the ground except for the mysterious Christian girl. Again and again, the earth shook. The upheaval split the temple floor and even tossed sand so high that it showered into the room through the open terraces. As abruptly as it had begun, the earthquake quieted.

Titus was sprawled on the floor still staring at the blurred figure of the Christian. She stood and ran away from the scene. "Wait," croaked Titus, but he could not bring his battered body to do anything more. The Christian did no such thing and disappeared into the corridors.

CHAPTER TWO

Titus' body quivered under the load he bore with each step. The metal-studded soles of his boots dug deep into the soft sand even as the blazing sun, unhindered by clouds, oppressed him from the sky. Titus' body was drenched in sweat, his throat and mouth parched. He absent-mindedly groped for his water skin somewhere within the clutter of the huge pack on his back.

He dared not break stride for even a few seconds for fear of a stupendously severe punishment from Valerius. Finally, he freed the water skin from its fastenings and felt a detached sense of security when its mouth touched his lips. He tipped his head back and felt instantaneous relief when the soothing water flooded over the dry flesh in his mouth. The water tasted sweet on his dry tongue and he gulped it down eagerly. When he finally drew the water skin away from his lips, he was alarmed at how depleted its store was.

Slightly shamed that he had so quickly drained the water from his supply, he kept his eyes forced ahead. Then he saw the head of the entourage. Valerius strutted forward with as much vigor as a well-rested athlete. He was the only one among them who did not display the telltale indications that he was reaching the limits of his beaten body. Valerius had never once touched his water skin and stayed the course without the briefest hesitation or complaint.

Titus precipitously felt his heel strike a stone and he tumbled forward. He struck the ground on his hands and knees, both of which sunk into the sand. As he balled his fists in frustration, he felt the fingers of his right hand close around a solid object. He extracted it from the sand to examine it. It was a small wooden cross, about the size of his palm. His first reaction was to discard it, but instead of doing so he stuffed it into his pack. Titus then clambered back to his feet, keeping his blistered face solemn and his aching body rigid and attentive. Titus resumed the march, perplexed by his discovery.

Several minutes passed until the legionnaires began to catch glimpses of dark figures in the distance, their appearance obscured on the horizon.

"The legion!" cried a legionnaire.

Valerius raised his arms over his head, shouting aloud. "Praise the gods we have returned!" he exclaimed. Many other legionnaires added their praises, and all of them were jovial and expectant of a moment's rest.

Twelve hours later, Titus sat suddenly upright on his cot. Cold sweat clung to his bare skin. He was breathing heavily and his sore, aching muscles were trembling. He reclined back stiffly onto the hard, uncomfortable surface. His head sunk back into the pillow and he tried to keep his eyes shut. His frenzied mind would not calm enough for him to slip into any sort of slumber again. And always reappearing into the forefront of his thoughts was the Christian girl who was saved by the earthquake. Why had she been so calm even when Valerius' sword was raised over her? Had she known what was going to happen? Again and again, Titus tried to disperse the thoughts, but to no avail. He had to find answers.

Titus had to know more about the Christos. He combed his memories for any knowledge of Him. He knew that fifty years before, the Empire had executed Him for His teachings, conspiring to rebel against the Empire. He had claimed He was the Son of the Jewish God. The Romans crucified Him, but His followers claimed that he rose again. Titus almost chuckled to himself. Nobody can escape death. But Titus could not bring himself to completely believe that. He had seen something that Rome could never explain. He could not deny that maybe the Christos, Jesus, had triumphed over death that day fifty years ago. Maybe His agonized death on the cross as He was scorned by all was not His end. The cross! Suddenly Titus remembered the small wooden cross he had removed from the desert hours ago.

He reached over to a small table at the side of his cot and picked up the cross there from where he had placed it earlier. Everything was beginning to make sense. Even as his mind began to align the events of the last two days and everything he knew of Jesus, a rage consumed him. He cast aside those ludicrous theories and hurled the cross away. First, he had to know more. He had to know the teachings of Jesus that could sway the wills of nations and frighten the mighty Roman Empire.

Titus rose from his cot and walked to the far side of the tent. He could hear the deep breathing of the seven other men in his tent. The legate, or leader of the legion, had put under Valerius' command a century of new recruits, to accommodate the drastic losses of the First Cohort, and replenishing the entire unit with new recruits. Valerius, Titus, and Herax were the only ones of the original century to have survived. Titus spotted his armor amongst that of the others. It stood out, for it was battered and horrifically damaged. Looking at it now, Titus realized how fortunate he was for being alive even now. He reached down and lifted up his gladius, the blade of which was concealed within its scabbard. Titus could only guess at the condition of the blade after the intense fighting, for he dared not unsheathe it for fear of waking his

THE VICTOR PART II

comrades. He then returned to his cot where he pulled a faded blue tunic over his head. He fastened a belt around his waist and attached to it the scabbard of the gladius. He shod his feet in his sandals and disappeared through the tent flap. The remnants of a fire smoldered a few yards away from Titus and the pale half-moon hung low in the sky. Titus turned north and began his trek. He strode briskly between the fabric walls of the tents, swaying gently in the breeze. For several minutes, he hurried about until he caught a glimpse of a human shadow cast across the darkened sand. He saw a javelin silhouetted in the man's right hand. A sentinel. A burst of panic sent adrenaline coursing through Titus' body from his chest. He set off at a sprint away from the sentinel. His feet fell silently into the sediment and flung dust into the air at his heels. His punished limbs struggled to propel him swiftly across the desert. Finally, he burst out of the perimeter of the camp and slowed himself as he began to rapidly approach the exterior trench that ringed the tents.

He forced himself to dash forward, willing his legs to move, to run, to jump. He planted his feet firmly on the other side of the trench an instant later. He swung his arms at his sides as he felt himself lean back over the trench despite his best attempts to stay his unbalanced swaying, and threatened to topple over. Finally, he found sure footing and bent over, his hands on his knees, as his chest swelled and shrunk with his labored breathing. Just as Titus turned to continue his journey, he saw the flash of steel speeding toward him in the darkness. He sidestepped and the blade whistled past his chest. Titus now saw the solemn, scarred face of the sentinel advancing on Titus with his spear held before him. Titus' hand fell to the familiar hilt of the gladius at his side, but before he could draw it, the sentinel sent the strong shaft of his spear into Titus' thigh with devastating force. Pain blossomed in his leg and in a flurry of dim motion, his face struck the sand.

He felt the metal studs in the soles of the sentinel's sandals being pressed against Titus' flesh as the sentinel ground his heel into Titus' back. Then Titus heard more footsteps, the culprit of which was drawing nearer. The pressure on his back vanished and rough hands pulled him to his feet. He was now gazing into Valerius' fierce eyes. "YOU FOOL!" bellowed the optio. He struck Titus' face with his palm, and the legionnaire recoiled, though refraining from doing anything more that would display weakness to his officer. Valerius gripped Titus' forearm and led him back to the camp. A small bridge spanned the trench, and Titus reluctantly crossed it at the prodding from Valerius. Titus lowered his head in humiliation and ground his teeth as Valerius forced him to the center of the camp. When they reached the circular clearing, Valerius forced Titus to his knees. Two legionnaires emerged from the darkness, each bearing a two-foot long length of rope. They fastened them around Titus' wrist, pulled them tight, and ushered him forward to the center of the clearing where there stood a ten foot tall wooden pole. Titus was reluctant to move, so the legionnaires dragged him through the sand. They wrapped Titus' arms around the pole and secured the two ends of the ropes on the other side. Titus now heard Valerius' voice behind him.

"You tried to desert! I could kill you, but no. Twenty lashes for your folly."

Titus' heart sank. His body would forever bear the mark of the whip. One of the legionnaires tore his tunic to expose his back. For several perilous seconds, Titus was left to his fearful thoughts and nauseated gut until he heard the whip crack. There seemed to be an abnormal gap between that quick sound and the white-hot burning pain that raced across his back. His body shook. He clenched his jaw and laid his head against the pole as he squeezed it with all his might between his arms. His eyes were welling with tears as the fire extended across his marred flesh. He was aware of the thin leather strip sliding across the sand as Valerius drew the whip back. Then came another swift pop. The tides of pain on the second strike merged with that of the first, washing over him and raking his body with agony that peaked and subsided like the lap of the sea on a quiet shore. Titus raised his head skyward. He screwed his eyes shut, every muscle he could control tightened. He opened his mouth slightly, though the muscles in his jaw remained rigid. His legs that had been holding him in a kneeling position now collapsed and he fell, writhing in agony to the ground. There was a crack. And another. Blood trickled down Titus' arms as he rubbed the skin raw on the rough wood of the pole. There was an all-consuming constant presence of incapacitating, awe-inspiring pain that radiated from his back. He was shaking drastically now. Another sharp noise brought on new rounds of fire. Titus' consciousness began to wane. The cracks of Valerius' whip continued. Titus was not aware of any individual strike now. He only knew that the pain never seemed to cease. Finally, the pain began to dissipate, leaving darkness to consume Titus' thoughts.

When Titus returned to consciousness, he was lying on his stomach on his cot, his back sore and stinging. Daylight was filtering through the thin fabric of the tent walls. To his left he heard a strong voice. Titus' mind slowly recognized the voice as that of the legate, or leader of their legion. It was a

THE VICTOR PART II

man by the name of Cornelius. "You are the luckiest young man I have ever seen."

"What?" questioned Titus.

"You bear no scars. The whip never cut into your flesh. You'll be sore as ever, but there's no permanent damage. It seems that you are blessed. To be among the only three in your century to survive yesterday's battle, and now to be unaffected by the whip, it seems that Mars has taken a particular liking to you. Maybe the same will hold true for those in your company. I am making you optio of your century and Valerius centurion. Your previous centurion, the noble Quintus, has been permanently stationed as an officer in the Praetorian legions in Rome. Your century will soon be sent to join them."

Titus suppressed a groan of depression. "Yes, sir," He muttered.

CHAPTER THREE
THE NEXT DAY

Titus was glad to be free of his cumbersome load as he let it drop onto the hard planks of the ship. Around him the other legionnaires were settling in amid the scum that plagued the lower deck for the long, arduous voyage ahead of them. From below came the slaves' groans of exertion as they heaved their exhausted bodies against the oars. Titus, like so many of his fellow Romans, detested traveling by ship, and was apprehensive of the next many days.

Titus then produced from the large pack a bedroll, which he laid out and sunk into. As Cornelius had said, his back was quite sore, but there was no serious damage and he was recovering swiftly. As always, when the legionnaire gained a moment of quiet, his thoughts fell to the matter of the Christos. Was it He who saved Titus from the damage the whip could have caused? *NO!* Titus told himself. He would no longer allow himself to be troubled by all this. He was much better off before he met the Christian girl. He screwed his eyes shut, and with every ounce of willpower he could muster, he allowed his mind to ignore, even if ever so briefly, the ubiquitous thought of the Christos, and drifted into a fitful sleep.

When Titus again woke, the shafts of brilliant daylight pouring in between the planks of the top deck were dimming. He sat up and inspected his surroundings. Many of the legionnaires were still in a deep slumber, some were pacing, and others were staring blankly ahead, and many more were gambling. They sat in small groups, their backs hunched, rolling dice repetitively between themselves. Titus found that his frustration with the Christos had not quieted and he theorized that gambling would take his mind off of it.

He spotted quickly the group in which Herax sat. Next to his friend, Titus saw a stout legionnaire grinning widely as he gathered the coins strewn between the players, sweeping them in toward where he sat cross-legged.

A grim sort of smile curved Titus' lips as he plunged his hands into his pack where it still rested next to his bedroll, lopsided due to its ungraceful descent. When his hand emerged a second later he held a small bag of rough fabric that fit in his palm. He shuffled over to Herax's group and sat down among them as they were preparing to start the whole process of the game over again. In the center of the ring of men were two dice and Titus knew that lives could change by their lot. Titus smiled feeling once again the exhilaration of risk. The others put forth their money and Titus produced multiple coins of his own. Three month's wages. "I'm in as well," Titus said, and the group rippled with murmured consent. Some who were obviously drunk didn't seem to know what was happening, but shoveled out their money with a disturbing lack of conviction.

Soon, the dice were tumbling across the deck and the small heap of coins in front of each participant slowly deteriorated. Within only a couple of minutes or so, Titus' pile had shrunk alarmingly only to be replenished by a surge of good fortune. And so the games proceeded for seemingly endless hours, until darkness swallowed the vessel and the gamblers plowed on by candle-light. Some of the soldiers retired to their bedrolls, but Titus, Herax and a few others remained the while. Just as the dice were being passed once again into Titus' hands, the darkness that had grown in the shadowy compartment was shattered by the light of a strong lamp. Titus whirled to see Valerius bearing the source of illumination as he descended from the deck above. He viewed the room, populated by the new recruits that had replenished his nearly decimated century, and then spotted Titus.

"You, Optio!" he shouted.

Titus rose as he was addressed. He had almost forgotten that he had been appointed second in command.

"Follow me," Valerius said, and disappeared back to the top deck. Titus trotted to the hatch and ascended, finding that his legs ached from his prolonged time on the floor. He quickly emerged onto the deck. He could feel the cool night air, and looking past the horizon he could see thousands of stars marking the deeds of past heroes. He saw Valerius, holding his lantern a dozen yards away, and made his way over to him. The boat pitched and shook in the waves and a powerful wind broke upon it, stinging any of Titus' exposed flesh with the cold bite. As Titus reached the centurion, Valerius gestured to the rigging beside him.

"Hoist the sail," Valerius ordered. "Maybe we can make some progress with the wind at our backs." Titus obediently took up the position and found a firm grip on the rough fibers of the proffered rope. He strained his muscles, heaving his body, but he made only a little headway in lifting the huge, heavy sail. However, in moments, other sailors had taken up positions on the sail rigging and together it was a simple matter to raise the massive piece of tough canvas. Valerius stood a few feet away, glancing appraisingly at Titus' efforts with his steely eyes. As the sail caught the strong wind, it swelled, and Titus felt with satisfaction the ship slowly gaining speed. He stepped away from the ropes when his task was complete, only to see a squat man beckoning to him from beside Valerius.

"I am Captain James Tiberius," the man said. Titus nodded and Tiberius continued. "Optio, as I was telling your centurion, this water is thick with pirates, and one of my sailors has just spotted an approaching ship. It's not answering our hails. It offers no indication of nationality or its purpose in these parts."

Titus hurried to the side of the ship, his heart beating faster. He stepped up on the railing of the ship and scanned the water around it. Sure enough, the massive object loomed only a couple hundred yards away. It was alarmingly close, but by far more disconcerting was its swift approach, and it offered no signs of altering its course as it plowed through the waves straight for the Roman galley. Titus saw the vast form of the monstrous thing. It dwarfed their ship, and if it was pirates, they were doomed. Just then, he saw a glint in the moonlight, and before he could think anything more, he saw an arrow speeding toward him from a high arc. He jerked his body away from it and the fletching brushed his face as it passed him. As it sped on and disappeared into the pitch black, it did something most strange. It clattered, as if striking stone. Titus' precarious footing on the ship's railing slipped and his body pummeled the deck as he fell. The wind was knocked out of him and he gasped in shock. To his right he heard a sailor's cry of, "Pirates!"

Titus did not panic or fear, but rather brightened with a fierce sense of anticipation. Anger had been swelling in him since the earthquake and he wanted nothing more than to expel Christ from his mind in battle. "Captain," Titus heard Valerius say, "Turn us aside!"

"I can't do that!" Tiberius said, pointing to the side of the ship opposite of the pirates. Valerius and Titus looked, to see a massive rocky mound of earth rising from the water, only a few dozen yards from the ship.

"Then we fight!" Valerius bellowed without hesitation. Titus clambered to his feet and dashed over to the hatch. He dropped down to the lower deck, all the while shouting that pirates were coming.

When he saw that few people were responding, he cried again with more urgency. "Pirates are here, you fools. Grab a sword, get up there, and fight!" Titus hurried to his pack and drew from it his gladius. He freed it from its scabbard and tossed the latter aside. The others were either doing the same or waking their sleeping comrades. Then, the ship drastically shook. It bore familiarity to the earthquake he had experienced a few days before. The side of the ship was bulging inward and then the planks shattered. Water rushed in, sweeping aside men and belongings alike that were scattered on the floor. In only a second it was about Titus' waist and he was close to being submerged. Others lost their footing and disappeared. Everyone who could was charging toward the hatch with the uttermost haste. Cold spray bombarded Titus as he ran. As he rose to the hatch, he glanced quickly back. The prow of a massive ship was busting through the side of the galley. Below him he heard slaves, shackled down, unable to escape, screaming before they were suddenly and disturbingly silenced.

As Titus came to the deck along with many of his fellows, arrows poured down from the ship. Titus was somehow unharmed, while several of his comrades collapsed. He saw Valerius a few feet away, bearing his gladius and tower shield. Tiberius was speaking to him in a panicked voice. "Even if the pirates don't kill us, we'll die when the ship goes down."

"Then we'll kill the pirates and take the ship."

Titus sprinted after Valerius as the centurion leaped onto the pirates' ship. Valerius pushed forward, using his shield as a battering ram and hacking barbarically with his gladius. Titus had almost reached the pirates' ship when one of its crew leaped out to meet him with a scimitar. The pirate, apparently from the Asian provinces, was garbed with a turban and long robes, though his agility seemed not to be affected. He swung out his sword, but Titus dove to the side. Titus retaliated with a thrust of his own, but his foe parried before the blade found its mark. The pirate swung his sword in a semicircle before bringing it upward at Titus with passionate ferocity. Before the metal could taste his flesh, the Roman sent his gladius darting out into the mass of robes, and the blade stopped. Both apprehension and a twisted sense of profuse satisfaction came to Titus as his foe toppled over, his warm blood bathing Titus' blade. He smiled, and felt the terrible joy of the kill, and the maddening thrill of war.

Even as the pirate fell the ship pitched to one side. One side of the vessel was sinking into the inky depths, and the side above the sea was being thrown to a dangerous tilt. Beneath the battling Romans and pirates yawned the deep. The sea's maw seemed to reach out and beckon Titus into the foreboding abyss that could only hold death. Great sheets of water dashed upon the deck of the galley, snatching men to their macabre fate in the cold embrace of the water beneath. Titus was swept down the length of the galley by a powerful arm, until his momentum sent him hurtling into the mast. He wrapped his arms around it and dangled over the slanting deck.

The galley was turning in the water, sinking and flipping onto its back at the same time. All the while, the prow of the pirates' ship was yet embedded, and the galley was being ripped to pieces. An arrow was suddenly lodged in the mast only inches from his head, and the momentary recoil nearly compromised his grip. Finally, he brought himself to a position where he could lay against the mast, breathing heavily. He looked up to the deck of the pirate ship, where the forty or so tenacious men that were left of the Romans battled fiercely with the swarm of pirates. The only battle between the two forces now was that of survival. Whoever took the ship took the only chance to live.

Titus still had his sword in hand, and knew that where his fellows were, where their battle was, he must be there as well. Standing half upon the deck and half upon the perpendicular mast, he prepared for the charge. He sprinted up the steep surface, winning out only a dozen yards or so until gravity pulled him back and he leaped for the railing. He slammed hard into it, and using it as a support, he was able to pull himself up over the shuddering, thrashing form of the galley as it twisted into the depths. As he clambered onto the pirate vessel the galley was nearly submerged. He found himself faced by a pirate who brandished a Greek sword. He hacked down at Titus' head, and Titus blocked on instinct. Then he directed his sword and swung down at the pirate's torso. The foe quickly parried with enough force to jar Titus' hands. He hardly managed to keep a hold on the sword. The legionnaire proceeded to cock his arm back and thrust hard at the pirate's head. The sea-faring thief forced aside his arm and prepared to land a swift blow of his own. But Titus was quicker. He whipped his blade back across at the pirate and slashed his neck.

Titus looked to the sky and saw a bright white moon. He was panting from his exertions. His mind was racing, his heart pounding. He was only offered a second to collect himself before he noticed footsteps charging him rapidly. He saw a huge, muscular Asian charging him with a spear. A maniacal thrust from him barely missed Titus' head, yet the Asian barreled on, straight into the Roman. He was thrown back hard, and with a burst of shocking pain and breathlessness, the small of his back hit the railing. The Asian wrapped his thick arms around Titus and without hesitation heaved Titus over the railing. He fell for a moment before he struck the deck of the galley ship. Stunned by the fall, he barely realized that the second he hit the deck he was racing down its length into the dark water.

He was only aware of himself slowly descending as the air in his lungs poured upward from his gaping mouth, gasping for oxygen that he could not reach. But with an effort partly of his will and partly of an instinct to survive, his arms moved, his feet kicked, and he swam like mad for the surface. The muscles in his throat and gut seemed to lurch as if his entire body was scrambling for oxygen. His head ached and his mind buzzed. Water was soon flooding into his mouth and nose. His sinuses stung with the cold. He could feel consciousness fleeing from his cloudy mind until his head broke the surface. He gasped for breath, feeling it bring clarity and strength to him.

Titus swam over to the pirate ship. He could still hear the cantankerous battle unfolding on the deck. Titus found to his delight he had somehow retained his gladius, and he jammed the blade into the caulking between planks, pulling himself out of the water with the sword. He repeated the process, slowly rising, until he was able to pull his soaked body onto the deck of the ship with tremulous arms.

To his chagrin, however, he was not granted even a second's repast. Three pirates, with long, thin swords were closing in on him. The blades darted quickly in and out around him, and his instinctive movement became sporadic as he attempted to evade the lethal weapons. Any time there was a gap he thrust with his own gladius. Any part of the bodies of his aggressors that was within his reach he took a stab at. He felt his short sword connect with one's thigh, and his foe collapsed. He hacked at the back and the pirate sprawled dead. The other two laid in on him, raining down even more ferocious blows. One bodily threw himself at Titus, sending one final, desperate jab at the legionnaire. Titus forced out his arm, pushing the tip into his chest as his foe fell upon him. The two stared at each other, one in shock, the other in grim satisfaction, their faces inches apart. Then, the pirate sank back. The remaining pirate leapt for the Roman that had slain his fellows. The two struggled in the brutal melee that ensued. Flashing blades slashed at the opponent, and by only a few inches each time were they avoided, and they locked themselves in the death struggle, to force the other down and drive cold iron into his heart. Titus' sword was drawing ever closer to his enemy's flesh. In a final burst of furious strength, Titus ripped the blade up across his enemy's chest. He fell back upon the deck and the battle haze clouded Titus' mind and consumed his heart.

Everything that was inside of Titus was released. Turmoil. Confusion. Rage. He sprinted at the epicenter of the battle, where he knew there was the thickest fighting. As he came close, he saw the dead bodies of Romans and pirates scattered around several pairs of battling men. A dozen Romans still lived, battling with thirty pirates. He saw that a few feet away, crowded against the railing behind tower shields were Valerius and Herax. The latter still clutched the Roman standard.

Titus' attention, however, was directed immediately to the man who was charging him with what looked to be a pickaxe. The man swung down and Titus found that his reaction was too slow. He expected to feel its cold bite on his flesh, to feel death surging upon him, but he was wrong. He had blocked with one of the bracers on his forearms in an action born of years of hard training, and the weapon had never landed the lethal blow. Titus ran his enemy through. The foe dropped, but a second opponent was already jabbing a spear his way. He nimbly darted to the side and sent the point of his short sword into the man's face. The spearman staggered away and Titus followed. The horribly exhilarated, bloodthirsty fighter Titus had become, seething with hatred and the tumult of battle followed the spearman, swinging his sword at his side. Then, as he saw his chance, he brought the blade down into the torso. The man was motionless, fallen to the deck.

At once, several of men were rushing on Titus from all sides. He saw limbs and blades and the shafts of weapons whirling around him. A sword tore across his chest and the butt of a spear caught him in the face. He saw an exposed neck and on instinct his arm swung in a flash. A man fell. He saw a gap in one man's guard and forced his sword into it. The man doubled over the blade, limp. Titus knew not what was happening in the mad rush, only that in those moments he fought like he had only fought on rare occasions before, matched against such odds that no thinkable skill or virtue could have saved a man. He fought with only the hope that fate would be kind to him. But even then he knew that if he were spared, it would not be fate to do such a thing. And so he fought like mad until he was the only one standing. He saw the bodies before him, and was surprised at how little he felt for the sight. He knew that what he felt he would feel eventually, but not in battle. He only knew, in a cold, calculative way that death was at his hands. He knew that his body was thoroughly punished by the intense fighting, and he knew it would fail him soon. He looked down at his sword. It and his arm were drenched in blood. The blade slipped from his fingers, and darkness swallowed him as he fell to the deck.

A few yards away, the knot of men around Valerius and Herax had thinned. More than a dozen dead were heaped up against their shields, almost all slain at Valerius' hand. Herax was shocked at his Centurion's fighting. Of all the soldiers in the Empire, he was the only one who had grown near to Quintus' prowess in battle. The three or four men that still menaced the two entrenched warriors stepped back and a pirate of imposing stature took their place. He was undoubtedly their leader, armed with a curved sword and garbed with a long tunic that billowed in the swift breeze rising from the sea. The captain struck at Herax's head, and the sword met the helmet with a sharp retort. The legionnaire sank to the deck, unconscious. Valerius pulled his arm out of the tower shield, casting the thing over the side of the ship, and gripped the standard. He quickly parried two blows and dove over the railing, into the sea.

THE VICTOR PART II

CHAPTER FOUR
EIGHT HOURS LATER

Valerius was stretched out upon his tower shield, swaying in the sea. His limbs, dangling from the shield, hung suspended just below the surface of the water. His breathing was ragged through his cracked lips, his face blistered by the ruthless sun. His hollow stomach rumbled, his head throbbed, and his body was deeply consumed by exhaustion. And yet, for every instinct of survival he would not let sleep come to him. Even a brief lapse in his will, already waning under his misery, would let consciousness consume him, and the sea would claim his body.

He rolled his head to the side to examine the golden form of the eagle. The Roman standard was tucked in the crook of his shoulder against the shield. The sight of it renewed his hope and determination. Once again, as he had done before, he put his aching fingers on the rim of the shield and with trembling arms, struggled to raise himself a little from the shield. He was embarrassed by his weakness. He scanned the horizon all around him with squinting eyes, and his gaze halted on a miniscule speck standing out on the massive expanse of churning turquoise waters and clear blue sky.

His heart lifted. "Oh, let it be Roman!" Valerius cried aloud. He lowered himself again to the shield and kicked his feet in the water. His arms swept through the sea at his sides. His muscles vehemently protested the movement but by sheer indomitable will he forced them into submission. He was resolute in his cause. He would not let the glory of Rome that had lived with he and his warriors die with them. If to do nothing more than save the precious standard and his honor, he would make it to Rome. And for that, he would not die now.

With his propulsion the shield began to glide forward over the water. Its wooden structure was surprisingly buoyant in the water and it soon began to move as well as a small boat. Its success was met by silent celebration from the Roman. His mind had been dulled by the hours of harsh punishment from the sea and sun, but it now sharpened in his pursuit of the vessel. His eyes never left it, his only hope of deliverance, and he never allowed his tiring limbs to stop moving. Gradually, pain swelled around him, and it would have reduced a lesser man to weep, but Valerius gritted his teeth and persevered. Each second of his venture became to him his entire world and he could scarcely think. So addled was his mind that all concept of time was lost to him. In

THE VICTOR PART II

retrospect he would realize that it was about two hours in pursuit of the boat, but as he lived through the ordeal it could have been years.

His chest heaved and he was slightly alarmed at the exertion he endured. And so proceeded his mad rush for deliverance from the sea until, as if in an instant, the boat was looming before Valerius. It was a trireme, and a ship of the Roman navy at that. "Praise Neptune," he exclaimed as loud as his distraught lungs would allow. "He has had mercy on me!"

A head appeared over the railing, and judging from his attire one would surmise him a mariner. He gazed disapprovingly at the man in the water. "By your tongue you are a Roman," he said, "but that has proved misleading before. So tell me, who are you?"

Valerius was irritable in his suffering and now his patience shattered. He bellowed at the marine. "I AM A CENTURION OF ROME! A SOLDIER OF THE SAME EMPIRE AS YOU! BUT YOU ARE OBVIOUSLY TOO STUPID TO SEE THAT, YOU FOOL!" The marine appeared taken aback by the outburst. "Have you heard of Quintus, the greatest among the great soldiers of the Empire, now leader of the Praetorian legions?" The marine nodded. "I am his friend and comrade. Now get me out of this horrid water and I'll tell you everything. Oh, and take this." He took the staff of the standard

53

and tossed it up to the marine who caught it in an outstretched hand.

The marine turned away from the railing and after a few moments a rope was lowered. Valerius took hold of one end, fighting through exhaustion and pain, and held on long enough to be raised onto the deck.

Titus' eyes slowly opened and into his vision burst the image of a roof of rough wooden planks. The golden light of a candle danced across the weathered surface. Next came to his senses waves of pain in the form of a nearly intolerable dull ache. Then, he felt the sway of the structure he was in and knew at once he was on a boat. As he collected himself and tried to rationalize his surroundings, the mystery of his whereabouts began to work its way into his thoughts. He willed himself to sit up and better view the place but his body was lethargic and practically unresponsive so he soon abandoned the thought of it altogether.

He was granted only a second more to puzzle over it all until to his mind came the memories he had been withholding from himself, perhaps by some subconscious refusal to accept it. All the woeful events that had befallen him rushed into his thoughts and he reeled at the terrible reality. By something akin to a spasm he was jerked upright. Pain came, but at first he did not know from where.

Battle. He felt himself sickened by the combat. He was only sixteen. He knew that boys who had once been his friends were still biding their time in the small Greek town that was so influenced by Rome that it seemed but a miniscule, cheap imitation of the city. He knew that they were still dreaming of the life of a soldier and all the glory to be won. Titus had been one of them, just more than a year ago, though it seemed like a lifetime. He had seen gladiators basking in the fame and fortune that came with their skill in dealing death; he had seen soldiers, war heroes, parading through the town, resplendent in the glory of Rome that seemed to hang around them wherever they went. So seduced was he by the prospect of the honor and greatness that was only attainable in his mind through fighting for the Empire of Rome that he had joined the legions, saying he was seventeen, two years older than he really was.

Now, by the wars that he had longed for, he was here. And he was morose. Why, now, had this happened to him? His head fell forward and he barely kept himself from weeping. The enormous task of quieting his mind and indeed his soul was only attained as he strained all his willpower to the cause. And then his thoughts came once again, as they always did, to the Christos. What had this issue, thrust suddenly into his life, become? Then, in repetition of all the times before, came the confusion that the matter stirred. Fury accompanied this, but with a powerful effort he forced himself into indifference.

He looked around the room as he attempted to scatter his thoughts with something of the physical world, and noticed that it was a small, simple compartment. Titus noticed a door on the opposite side of the square room just as it was opened. It was a tall man that entered, and Titus realized he had seen him before, guessing that he was the captain of the ship. His breath slowed and his chest tightened. The look on the man's face told of his intentions, and his balled fist and stance ready for swift movement only offered validity to the inference. The man's wary eyes examined the Roman where he sat hunching awkwardly on the floor and Titus could only imagine what state his body must be in. The captain lunged at him before offering any explanation at all of the assault. Titus saw his quick and lethal movements and knew what was coming to him before he was even struck, and it terrified him. It was a unique fear, fleeting but deep-set, that can only be felt in a moment of rushed action as one awaits unavoidable pain.

The man was upon Titus and in an instant his tight fist darted out with devastating speed and strength. A dull thud sounded as the fist connected with Titus' chest and tossed him up against the wall behind him before he slumped forward onto the

THE VICTOR PART II

floor again. His sore face hurt as it was flattened against the hard wood, and he could not draw a breath. All the while, a putrid grin crept across the captain's face as he looked down at Titus.

He spoke down to his captive in a foreign language that seemed to Titus then quite vile. The man paused, awaiting a response, but when nothing of the sort came from Titus, he reached a realization. "Ah, Latin," he said, and started again, but his accent was thick and only added to his villainous demeanor.

"I am Savan," he said, "captain of this ship."

"What are you going to do to me?" Titus asked him, though speech was a struggle.

"You came to me under rather unsavory circumstances." Savan snarled at the recent memory. "I don't really know what I'm going to do with you, but I might kill you. I really have no use with you. Your leader, the centurion, got away with the standard, and is probably dead at the bottom of the sea right now, but that eagle was the only thing that would have given me a good profit. You could make a good slave, but eventually someone will find out you're a Roman citizen, so I'll have to choose the buyer carefully."

Titus wondered about Valerius, and how he had fared in the sea. He wished he himself had jumped overboard rather than falling captive to the pirates.

Savan grabbed hold of Titus' tunic and pulled up the Roman. He heaved him against the wall, hard, and then slung him bodily back to the ground. Titus was incoherent of his thought and his actions were slow and hampered by the protests of his throbbing muscles. Once again Savan yanked Titus to his feet, and when he slumped, he wrapped an arm around him. Savan heaved his prisoner out the door of the small room and throughout the bowels of his ship. They entered another small room, but here two people crouched in the straw that littered the floor. One was a Roman, Titus' comrade, well-muscled and glowering at Savan as he entered. He let Titus fall to the floor and met the calm eyes of the second, a young girl about his age.

Numerous minutes passed, the time prolonged by the discomfort of his present state, before Titus aroused from his stupor and stirred, abandoning his position sprawled on the floor. He looked up to the face of the girl, and was startled by the recognition. It was the Christian that had so troubled him since the day of the earthquake. The subject of his wonderment did not display the same realization, and Titus was suddenly aware that his face must be swollen beyond her recognition. With some difficulty, he spoke to her.

"Do you remember me, from the stronghold where we battled the Jews? I spoke to you."

The girl looked away in silence.

"What's your name?" Titus asked.

"Julia."

Titus leaned against the wall and looked over to the Roman on the opposite side of the room. "Herax?"

"Titus?" the standard-bearer inquired. His voice was not as weak as his comrade's and exhaustion did not cloud his demeanor as much as it did Titus'.

"Yes."

"I thought I was the only one who survived." Herax's face moved forward into the dim light. It was bruised and gaunt, but lightened slightly with hope. "You look awful."

"Yeah, I took a beating." There was a pause in the conversation. "Savan says Valerius dove over the side of the ship with the standard," Titus continued. "He thinks he's dead, but we both know Valerius wouldn't let that happen. He would find a way to survive, and save the eagle."

"Maybe he will find Romans and take down these accursed pirates. He will surely seek to avenge the deaths of his men."

Again there was quiet as the two silently imagined their centurion returning with a ship and an army and putting an end to the marauders. Julia looked at the blank wall between the Romans. She was sympathetic of their plight, but ever in her mind lingered the thought that it was men like these that hunted her and all Christians. When the conversation resumed, it grew to matters of increasing triviality. Time passed until two brutal-looking pirates, Asian by appearance, entered.

"Captain Savan has given orders that you be escorted to the top deck," one said. They ushered Titus and Herax out of their room and through a labyrinth of narrow, cramped hallways to the hatch door. They rose in single file, the captives going first, onto the deck above. Titus thought he could make a run for it once he emerged from the hatch, but he found immediately that he was surrounded by at least a dozen pirates, Savan among them. All four of the entourage were soon on deck with the captain and he spoke to the Roman captives.

"While you are on my ship you shall work for me. These men," he gestured to the pirates around him, "are free to order you two about as they wish. Disobey, and I will slit your throats and cast you to the sea."

Savan left and the pirates wasted no time ordering Titus and Herax to the rigging where they began their work. Titus heaved at one of the heavy ropes as ordered by the pirates, but he found that his body flared with pain and his sore muscles were unable to move it. His body had endured in the past few days two battles, a whipping, and he had been beaten by Savan. He was not surprised to find his body unresponsive, but as time passed, he began to adjust to the work and was soon able to function normally. They spent the remainder of the day indulging the pirates and laboring the most mundane and rigorous chores of a sailor. It was difficult work, supervised by unruly, savage men, but Titus was able to find solace in the monotony it repeatedly lapsed into.

When the day of work was over, Titus and Herax were sent back to their cell. Julia was still there. The three were silent for a long time. Titus was still conflicted by the matter of the Christos, which Julia had brought up days ago. If there was anyone he could ask it would be her, so, steeling his will, he spoke. "Tell me of Christ."

She looked at him and smiled slightly. "I can only tell you my story and what He has done for me. I know little else." She spoke quietly, but there was strength and conviction in her words. Her story was brief, but Titus was amazed. She told him of how she had heard a man preaching about Christ one day outside of Rome, for, to Titus' surprise, she had once been a Roman. She had gradually begun to believe, and to pray to Jesus. Then, the truth came to her suddenly, as if a curtain was being ripped from the world and she could see that she believed, fully. She travelled to Judea, worshipping, to see the land blessed by God. After she had met Titus in the temple stronghold, she had boarded a cargo ship which had been overtaken two days from port.

Finally, she told Titus of her faith in Christ. She knew God and His Son in ways words were scarce enough to describe. She felt Jesus' comfort when she was persecuted, and when her faith wavered, as it did often in trials, she prayed, and when the Holy Spirit came again she praised God wholeheartedly. "I learned a prayer," she said, "from the preacher outside of Rome. He said it was the prayer Jesus taught to his disciples."

"Can I hear it?" Titus requested.

"Our Father who art in heaven, hallowed be thy name. Thy kingdom come, thy will be done, on Earth as it is in heaven. Give us this day our daily bread and forgive us our trespasses as we forgive those who trespass against us. Lead us not into temptation but deliver us from evil. For thine is the kingdom, the power, and the glory forever. Amen." Each word was spoken with such truth and devotion that it struck Titus to the core.

With the prayer filling his mind, he turned away from Julia and drifted to sleep.

The next morning when he awoke, he found Herax already awake, happy and excited. "I believe, Titus!"

"What?"

"I prayed. I felt God, I don't know what happened. I don't know anything except that I believe!" Julia, too, was awake, and was nodding along with Herax as he spoke.

THE VICTOR PART II

A few minutes later, Titus and Herax were led back to the top deck where they continued their work as they had the day before. When they returned to their room, they recited the prayer with Julia, but Titus lacked the fervor of the other two. The other days continued in the same fashion, and Titus became accustomed to the exertion of the labor. And every time he prayed, he felt something, surely the Holy Spirit, tugging at him to believe. But he refused, for he knew that if ever he escaped the pirates, there was still a life waiting for him, and he knew that if he accepted Christ he could never seek the life that every Roman strived for.

ANDREW MEADE

CHAPTER FIVE

The days on the boat became weeks, and as time passed slowly and steadily, Titus thought often of escape and vengeance against the pirates. He craved it. One day as he walked across the deck to his next job under the wary eye of a particularly narcissistic and unsavory pirate, he heard one of the sailors speaking to Savan. He caught only a fraction of the conversation, but it was enough. "Only a day to shore…" the sailor said. Titus' heart soared. That night, after their prayers, he informed the other two of the news.

"Valerius, I suppose, will be too late."

"Maybe not," Titus offered, feigning hopefulness. "And even were he not to come, it would doubtless be easier to escape on land."

Julia now spoke. "If we don't escape, and Savan sells us as slaves, we will most likely never see each other again. But we can never lose faith in Christ."

Titus hardly refrained from scoffing at her. He could not think about that now. He valued it little to the more pressing matter of his circumstances in the physical world. He retired himself from the conversation, his mind working quickly. The pirate vessel must be swift to traverse the Mediterranean in a week less of the time a Roman ship would require. Despite his inability to formulate a sufficient plan of escape, he fantasized about freedom and his life as a true Roman once again. In all of this, Christ was forgotten.

When he awoke the next morning, he was anxious for the day. Before his eyes were even opened, a tight grip clamped down on his shoulder and jarred his body. He looked up into the face of one of Savan's crewmen, pulled tight in an expression denoting his attempt to hide his distress. "To the oars, slave," he said. As Titus was hastily sent to lower deck, he was puzzled by the word spoken to him by the pirate. *Slave.* Never once on the boat had he been referred to as a slave, nor did he think of himself as anything other than a captive. But now he was a slave of the pirates, and his freedom was not to come.

While being led to the oars, he saw out of an open hatch the faces of the crew above. They were faces of awe and surprise. They stared blankly at the distance, and as Titus spotted what they were staring at, he almost smiled. It was a ship, moving steadily toward them, and it flew the colors of the Roman navy. *Valerius!* He was fairly intoxicated with glee, after lacking it for so long. He offered the matter little thought and lacked any resistance as he was seated at one of the benches to the oars, and was shackled securely. He took up the oar without hesitation as he was ordered to do so, though he really didn't know what he was doing. He plunged the oar into the water at the beat of the drum, heaved against it, removed it from the sea, and held it poised over the water for a moment before repeating the process even as the drum beat a second time. The nearly two dozen other slaves, whom he had scarcely noticed throughout the voyage, except for Herax who was among them, also tore through the water, and the speed of their already swift vessel doubled as the power of the oars was added to that of the wind.

The ship plowed through the waves with a speed that Titus had never experienced in a ship, and he finally came to the realization that had before eluded his befuddled mind. They were fleeing from the ship, and they feared another battle with their already weakened crew. He would have gladly released his oar and abandon the effort to all the better ensure his escape, had he not feared the wrath of the pirates. He consoled himself however, by knowing that Valerius would go to any means to intercept the object of his pursuit, and he would surely be free by dusk.

Minutes passed, and his arms tired till the task of moving his oar once more was painful and difficult. An hour passed, but to Titus it seemed most of the day. And so he continued, growing ever more pessimistic. But then, as he was quite sure Valerius would not come, he heard a great din from above. Men shouted as they rushed about on the deck above, and then there was a great roar as a wave was shattered by the bow of a ship. But it was not Savan's ship. The Romans were upon them.

An immense tremor racked the ship from the far end and Titus looked back to see the planks bending under great stress. The oar was jerked from his hand and its splintered remains fell at his feet as the boat shattered the wood as it passed. Not even a minute later all the noise of battle filled his ears and he knew the Romans had boarded the ship. Titus knew not how long the battle raged, but he was enthralled by it, listening every second, and aware always that his fate depended on the outcome. Shackled to their benches, he and the other slaves were helpless, and observed the battle only through the sound of it and brief flashes of motion seen through an open hatch near the end of the compartment.

After the battle had endured for a long while the Romans withdrew from the ship and resumed their original action of ramming the vessel with the prow of their trireme. With a devastating blow, Savan's ship capsized and tumbled onto its side. A dozen or more of the hull's planks shattered on impact and the sea water, foaming and churning, rushed in. As the boat rolled, Titus fell from his bench, and his rapid descent was halted abruptly and painfully as the chain of his shackle reached its extent. He dangled there from one leg, looking frantically around, until he saw the prone body of a pirate fall through the open hatch, a gladius embedded in his midriff. The deceased marauder slid down the aisle between the benches, and as he passed Titus where he hung inverted, the captive reached out and took hold of the sword's hilt. He wrenched the blade from the pirate and felt a sense of relief at the familiar feel of the weapon.

He hacked at the chain again and again until one of the links broke, and he dropped from the chain. He hit the hull and rolled down along its contour until he was stopped suddenly as he struck a bench on the opposite side. He still held the gladius as he came to his feet and spotted Herax. He sprinted over to him. He knew it was selfish to save Herax rather than anyone else, but was unable to risk the life of his friend. The other slaves shouted in dismay at him as he offered them no assistance. As he reached Herax, he set about hacking with his sword at the chains.

But it was to no avail. The ship rocked violently a second later and more water rushed in. Titus lost his footing and disappeared into the torrent. He clambered against the force of the swirling water, trying to push his head above the surface, to go back and save his friend, but he was not strong enough and was only swept away. He lost himself in the water as it dragged him along. All the while, he would not surrender his grip on the gladius, though it could help him little now. As he swam like mad, he opened his eyes enough to see faint figures through the swirling water. He was aware faintly in the back of his mind where he was in the flooded compartment, and as he neared the wall, he positioned himself and braced his muscles to take the impact with his legs. But he underestimated the force of the water, and while he took the force as he slammed into the wall, it ripped his feet away and dragged him through the hole where the Romans' battering ram, on the prow of their trireme, had shattered the timbers of the boat. His thoughts were of Julia and her well-being amid the chaos before his head broke the surface of the water and he gasped desperately for air.

He emerged into turmoil of tossing waves. Oars whirled around his head, and he saw that only a few yards away there loomed above him the massive Roman ship. He dove back under the water and swam away from the reach of the perilous oars. When he resurfaced, he was amid scattered wooden debris in the water. Titus saw a blur speeding toward him and ducked as a javelin, hurled from the Roman ship, sped over his head. The javelin disappeared in the water behind him as Titus reeled, aghast that his own fellows would attempt to kill him. He saw Valerius holding a bloodied sword and pointing to Titus in the sea. Archers nocked arrows and drew back their bows.

Titus plunged back into the water as the missiles were released. He saw the skeleton of the pirate ship hanging suspended in the water below the surface. Below it, slowly descending in the water, was a human figure, struggling against the weight of the object to which it was bound. Titus needed only a second to recognize the person. He dove after Julia, swimming rapidly. The exertion tore oxygen from his lungs, but he finally reached her, unwilling to draw back from the pursuit. He saw that her ankle and foot were caught in a tangle of netting around a heavy trunk of some kind. He carefully but quickly severed the netting with his gladius and wrapped an arm around her, to keep her from sinking yet lower. His chest ached in longing for oxygen and he knew that she must be in a worse state than he.

They were easily thirty feet below the surface, and as Titus looked up he could see little more than a faint glow from the radiant sun through the depths of the ocean. Titus nearly panicked at the thought of Julia's life, fearing that he could not save her from drowning in time. The rest of the hurried ascension to the surface seemed only a swarm of confusion and fear till Titus felt cool air dashing against his skin and, breathing deeply, looked over to see Julia taking great gulps of the sweet oxygen. "Thank you, Titus," she said, smiling in relief. Titus nodded. He reached a plank of wood and Julia laid herself over it. Titus eyed the Roman boat warily for a time before deciding they were at a safe distance.

Then, in a silent exclamation, a thought came rushing back to him. *Herax!*

Titus saw on the horizon a dark mass of land and told Julia to go to shore. She opened her mouth to protest his command, but he stopped her. "Please. Just go.'

There was a second's hesitation, but she finally lowered herself over the length of wood and paddled away from Titus. Titus sank back below the water and swam over to the remains of the pirate ship. When he reached it, he pulled himself through the hole and into the rower's compartment. What greeted his eyes was a terrible sight that would haunt him for months. He was the only one who escaped. The others were drowned, floating eerily in the dark water, still tethered to their benches. He saw Herax and his throat and chest tightened. He swam over to his friend, emotions in a tumult. He broke the chain and wrapped Herax in a melancholy embrace to keep hold of him as he swam upward with swift kicks. He nimbly braced his foot against the timbers and kicked out to propel them through one of the holes in the hull. Titus was sorrowful as they rose through the water, and when they broke the surface, the only thing that kept him from weeping openly over the death of his friend was the awful circumstances in which he found himself entrenched.

Titus drew close a barrel bobbing in the water and with difficulty heaved Herax onto the object of precious buoyancy. As he did so, Titus caught sight of his friend's face, pale and gaunt, jaw slack, eyes wide, and it terrified him until he nearly lost his wits. He sank back as the guilt came rushing on him, with a strength that made it seem a physical force ripping his mind apart. He could have saved him. He could have cut Herax free before the water swept in. Titus clenched his jaw, reminding himself of what was happening right now. For now, Herax's death could mean nothing. Later he could mourn and settle his conscience, but for now he could not let it impair him. So, he forced himself into indifference. Titus propped himself up on the floating barrel. He closed Herax's eyes and rolled the disturbing face away from him. Suddenly, a noise roared behind him and he whirled around to look.

He looked to see the Roman ship, oars in swift movement, swinging the trireme around violently to face him. With a speed that sent Titus' limbs burning with pumping adrenaline it rushed across the water in his direction. He kicked and paddled furiously but the barrel on which he was perched was frustratingly unresponsive. Even the faintest hope he had of seeking refuge with the Romans was dashed by their hostility, and he doubted that he could ever convince them he was a Roman before they killed him. Yet the instinct of self-preservation inspired him to try to seek refuge with the people he had long dreamed of as his rescuers. "I'm a Roman!" he bellowed. He once again spotted Valerius among the armed men on deck and shouted again. "It's me, Titus! I'm a Roman! I'm a legionnaire!" But nothing became of his desperate screams, and the trireme was hurtling for him so horribly fast that for an instant he was frozen in a rush of fear. But for only a moment he was so, before he returned to his senses. Acting hastily, he gathered up Herax and plunged into the rolling waves as the trireme rent the water above his head. The prow swung perilously close, but the vessel passed, and Titus was safe.

Titus arose again, and though the debris was scattered in the ship's wake, he quickly managed to situate himself and Herax on a plank, and followed the path Julia had taken, leading toward the shore. Though he was tired and sore from his exertions and frequent periods without air beneath the sea, he maintained his pace and made steady progress across the expanse of water. He refrained from looking upon Herax, for each time the sight redoubled his sadness, despite his best efforts to suppress it. After more than an hour, the waves churned beneath him, and, tossed from the plank, he and Herax fetched up on the shore. He pulled Herax away from the tide and glanced at the body. He could not imagine his friend's terror as water flooded into his lungs. He had seen hundreds die on the battlefield, but this was different. It racked his soul with terrible grief and a rush of emotions, and he found himself wholly miserable.

The Roman stood and examined the shore. His bones and muscles ached, but he refused to sink back down as he longed to do. The sandy shore continued for a few hundred yards away from the water before the landscape gradually shifted into rolling green hills. Looking down the length of the beach he spotted a figure almost a quarter-mile away. He hoped it was Julia, but was uncertain. He retrieved his gladius from the shallow, rippling water and set off towards the figure. In a matter of minutes he neared it, and alas, it was Julia. He shouted to her, but she did not respond. Her eyes were fixed upon a man approaching from the shallow water. She turned and fled suddenly, and as the man gave chase, Titus recognized him in a grim and alarming realization. It was Savan; he bore a scimitar and had the look of a madman on his face as he ran after Julia.

THE VICTOR PART II

Titus brandished his gladius as he charged at him. Even as he leapt for the pirate, swinging around his short sword in a wide, powerful arc, the latter lunged for Julia. Savan brought up his scimitar just in time to stop the deadly blow. Even so, Titus slammed into him. They staggered away from the collision, before simultaneously lowering themselves into battle stances. They were poised to deliver a furious onslaught of blows at any moment. At once, they both advanced and swung their swords overhead at the other. The blades met in the middle of their arc and spewed sparks. Titus quickly disengaged before his foe, with a longer reach, could drive his blade forward and into his heart. The pirate immediately assailed the Roman with masterful blows. The attack was furious, and the lethal, dancing blade darted close to the target many times. Titus, desperate to survive, threw his weight into every movement, and committed so fully to every powerful blow that he was reckless and on the verge of defeat at every second. His blood burned at the sight of Savan, and his arm struck out with the strength of his great anger, his blade moving at the whim of his unbound rage. Finally, one of Titus's savage thrusts promised to strike home at the heart, and he lunged into the attack. Savan recoiled, and bringing up his blade, swung it quickly at Titus' exposed chest. The Roman withdrew his blade but scarcely parried in time.

The blades met and rasped against each other, and the fighters drove them ever closer to their opponent. Titus put his left hand on the pommel of his short sword and strained against the strength of Savan and his two handed weapon. Soon, the blades locked at the hilt, and it was a contest of strength alone as neither opponent yielded. They dug their feet into the loose sand and strained against the other. They struggled fiercely, trying to force their blades into one another. Savan roared, his face contorting in fury. Then, in a jerking motion, the pirate captain stunned the Roman with an elbow blow to the gut and knocked the gladius from his grasp. Titus hastily gathered himself up again and fastened his grip on Savan's forearms. The pirate's eyes blazed. Savan snapped his wrist around, swinging his sword as effectively as he could within the constraints of his opponent's hold. Titus leaned away to avoid the sword, bending his face toward the sky as the blade sped centimeters from his nose. Titus' balance wavered, and as Savan pushed him hard to send him sprawling, he kicked one foot around into the back of his enemy's knee; they both toppled.

The shore was sloped, and the two tumbled down the slope, locked in a martial embrace, each trying to gain the advantage on the other as they struggled within the hold. They grappled with the scimitar as the blade jerked back and forth, drawing blood as it struck. Titus finally disengaged from the pirate, and as he rolled away, Savan struck out at him with balled fists. The blow never landed, and as he fell, his outstretched arms were struck over a boulder jutting from the hill with an unnerving *crack.* The scimitar fell from his hand and Savan tumbled down the face of the boulder, while Titus retained a position at its top. Savan was at a lower, less ideal position, nearer the pulsing sea. They both came to their feet. Savan reached for the scimitar, and Titus leaped down from the boulder, wrapping his arms around Savan and tackling him before he could retrieve the sword. Titus knelt over Savan, punching him savagely. But Savan was only angered. He sent a brutal uppercut into Titus' face, vision bursting red and yellow, and rammed his knee into his ribs. Titus was flung onto his back as Savan bucked underneath him, and sprawled on the sand, clutching his side and streaming blood from his face. Savan scrambled over to Titus, pinning him to the ground, and clutching his face, thumbs moving for the eye sockets. Titus, knowing Savan's intentions, threw up his own hands, struggling to pull away Savan's deadly grip. He felt the thumbs groping near his eyes, and a second later a burst of agony flared in his skull and he thrashed helplessly beneath Savan.

Finally, Titus pitched upward desperately, and for a second, Savan's hands slipped away.

Twisting his body and beating at the pirate, Titus clambered away from him. For a second he stood, gasping and clamping his hands over his eye sockets. But he was forced to face his foe again when Savan charged him, shrieking like a devil. Titus threw himself into Savan. Limbs battered bodies as the two fighters pummeled each other. Titus held his own, receiving the massive blows of his enemy and retaliating with his own. Yet Savan was too powerful. He beat Titus mercilessly until all coherent thoughts left the Roman. Then, grabbing his tunic, he slammed him up against the boulder hard. Titus frantically kicked out at Savan's midriff, and the latter staggered away. Then, falling to his knees, Titus grasped the hilt of the scimitar, still lying where it had fallen. Savan fell upon him once more, fist cocked back, and Titus swung up the blade, burying it to the hilt beneath Savan's armpit. He collapsed where he was. An awful wavering moan escaped his trembling lips. For a second he thrashed violently, and then he was still. Savan was dead.

Julia approached, gasping as she saw Titus. His body battered, Titus slumped against the boulder, and muttered one word. "Herax." He raised one shaking arm and pointed to where he had left his body. Titus raised himself from the boulder and staggered in the direction. Julia ran over to him, taking one of his arms around her shoulders and helping him walk. Her teary eyes were fixed on the figure of Herax lying in the sand. When they reached him, Titus collapsed, and Julia fell sobbing over the prone body. As he looked at the two, he cursed to himself for the trivial thought that entered his mind. *Jesus.* Julia believed. Herax had believed. And somewhere, deep in his heart, Titus could not ignore the fact that he believed too. He had to hope that his friend's faith meant something, that Herax had not died with faith in an empty God. And somehow, he knew that he hadn't. His world was shattered. Everything he had ever known was in turmoil. But suddenly, one thing was clear. There was one truth, that he could no longer deny. Slowly, he began to utter a prayer. And never had he prayed so intensely. He could almost feel the presence of God. His God. "Our Father who art in heaven," his heart lifted in warmth, "hallowed be thy name… Thy kingdom come, thy will be done, on Earth as it is in heaven… Give us this day our daily bread and forgive us our trespasses as we forgive those who trespass against us… Lead us not into temptation but deliver us from evil… For thine is the kingdom, the power, and the glory forever. Amen." In between each phrase he paused, as the truth and significance struck deep in his heart. Jesus had said the same words.

He looked up to Julia, and saw her smile slightly. "I—believe," he said, and laughed suddenly. "Come," he said. "Let us bury our friend further inland. Titus dragged the body up the shore, straining, until the ground was covered with sparse grass and vegetation. There, with their hands, the two dug a shallow grave for Herax. Reverently, they placed the body in the earth and pushed the loose dirt over it. "We will leave Savan to the Romans," Titus said. He retrieved his gladius, and together he and Julia headed into the hills.

THE VICTOR PART II

CHAPTER SIX
TWO WEEKS EARLIER IN ROME

Adir was sprawled on his back upon the rough, hard stone of the cell in which he was imprisoned. Around him, along the cracked plaster of the floor were a few small piles of filth that had accumulated throughout the cell's many years of negligent tending. One wall of the room was of dark iron bars through which he had a view of the gloomy corridors around him. Adir's head throbbed. His body ached terribly and in some places burned as if a white-hot brand was being thrust upon it. A few of the wounds actually had been formed in that fashion the previous day.

Playing across Adir's mind was the horrid memory of the time in the arena. Yet amidst the despair that was welling inside of him, he had a shard of hope, or rather joy in the remembrance that God, the God of Israel and indeed all the world, father of Christ, his God, had saved him. And not the first time, for many miracles had preceded it, and now Adir knew he must fulfil his promises. He must serve Him.

His eyelids, which had been closed for hours, were urged to move again. As the veil of darkness over his vision receded, he caught sight of the ceiling. Its familiarity and simplicity elicited a feeling, a yearning that had been buried when his journey began, after he had escaped the ludus. He longed to live with the luxury and whimsy of those who claimed him as their property, who ruled his life as if it were utterly insignificant, as if it had been brought into this world for their sake only, not that of the human being itself. The thoughts brought back into him a searing, consuming rage that he had abandoned for almost five months. It clouded out any other sensible thought and seemed to be burning away at him until it would break free and destroy him. His whole mind, his whole strength was devoted to a single moment of fury at those who had taken his world away, before it even began. As the waves of anger subsided after a while, as they always did, he quieted his anger with what few consoling words he remembered from Matthias.

Adir heard the commotion of the arena above him. He knew that innocent people were being slaughtered to entertain the mob. He heard the muffled voice of the announcer, calling out to the audience. He heard the clatter of swordplay and was fairly certain that gladiators were battling. Their battle began to adopt a rhythm, and Adir could visualize clearly the movement they made, one sword darting or hacking forward, to be parried or sidestepped by the opponent. But the pace of the fight was soon shattered with no pretense. The swords never met this time. He heard the death cry of a gladiator and a solid thud as he hit the ground.

The audience gasped audibly and then erupted into enthusiastic applause, or jeering from the ones who had apparently lost a wager. Adir could hear little more until the sound of metal grinding against stone signaled the gate being opened into the corridor outside his cell. Two pairs of footsteps entered, closing the door behind them, and growing ever closer to Adir. He could hear them dragging a heavy object between them, and a deep voice boomed out even though he only spoke. One said, "He was clumsy. Weak. Nearly everyone counted on him dying, and when he slipped up once, a lot of good bets were won, I'll say." The other mumbled an agreement. But Adir immediately knew the voice of the one who spoke, and was revolted at it. Quintus.

Presently, the two men passed his cell. They were both soldiers, as Quintus would always be, but they were differently attired than the ones that fought on the frontiers of the empire. They were elite, from the Praetorian legions, for Quintus had been appointed as an officer at the head of several such legions, under direct command from the emperor. The tunic Quintus wore under his armor was of a deep purple, and his apparel displayed regality. And between the two soldiers, like harbingers of war and death, they carried a dead body, limp in their arms. They moved to the edge of Adir's vision and together heaved the body out of sight. Adir heard the body slap onto the hard ground, where it would be attended to by slaves at a different time. Quintus puffed in satisfaction. Quintus then turned to Adir's cell staring intently at the one lying there, severely wounded and near death. He leaned in close to the bars and whispered venomously, "I'm surprised you're still here. You have fatal wounds and we threw you in here to die, but you're still with us. All the better, I say. I want to drain any life, or emotion, or hope or faith out of you."

With that, Quintus left.

Adir rolled back his head and slipped into unconsciousness once again.

A sharp noise startled Adir from his stupor just before daybreak that night. A faint, wavering orange glow told him there was a torch about a dozen feet from his cell. His body was in a state of agony that he had previously thought unattainable. Every joint ached as if his bones were being shattered again and again every second. It felt as if his insides were boiling. And his skin seemed to be shredded all over again. He would have cringed, had his stiff muscles allowed him to, at the thought of all that Bacchus and the lions had put him through. And yet in the moment he had noticed little more than scratches and soreness in his muscles.

He knew he should be dead. He knew as well that the fact he was alive now, even in the state of his wounds, was a miracle. He tried hard to remind himself what he had done it all for, Christ. But his thoughts were slipping. His heart was in pieces. It was all so much. In a few months everything was changed and crumbling in on him. And he knew more than anything of the misery that awaited him. So why was God keeping him alive? Wouldn't death be the merciful thing now? *Please Lord,* he prayed, *take me home to You now. I can do nothing more for you here, and I beg you not to make me face what it will incur to serve you. I do not want that pain. Please, take this burden from me.* Then, a soft urging entered his heart. It was not in coherent words, but just in ideas, emotions and, above all, truth, moving in his heart and mind and pulling him away from his pleading for death. His mind then formulated words to present the feeling. They came to him not of his own accord, but as if they were spoken to him through the silence.

No, it said. *Wait. Follow God. Do everything you can to serve Him, and trust Him with the rest. He will bring you to so much more than this, in time.*

Adir was encouraged by the words and cherished them in his heart, determined to hold fast to their truths in whatever followed. Even as he concluded this, he heard the same sharp noise that had awoken him and was filled with dread as familiar footsteps were followed by Quintus sauntering into the room. In his right hand was a metal bar, the tip of which was glowing red-hot. Adir realized what was happening and desperate tears filled his eyes. He never sobbed, but his chest was moving quickly, and his mind was eclipsed in fear.

Quintus wore no armor now, but he was still clothed in his fine purple tunic. He produced a key from his leather belt and unlocked the cell door, swinging it open loudly and addressing Adir with a cold, hard voice. "Still you escape death." He said with a lopsided, maniacal grin. "That will change tonight."

Quintus raised his leg and rammed his foot swiftly onto Adir's side. The captive let out a shuddering breath as pain laced his torso. "Why?" Quintus asked simply. Adir was unresponsive, and the Roman continued nevertheless. "Why do you devote your life to a God whose existence you are unsure of?"

"I am not unsure," Adir said, though his words were faint and labored. Quintus let the glowing tip of the bar he held drop onto the bare flesh of Adir's

THE VICTOR PART II

left arm. Adir's throat constricted with the pain and he choked as he tried to take in breath. A smile played across Quintus' lips as he looked down at the boy and he lifted the bar finally. Adir's body, which had been convulsed in the agony, went limp again.

"But how do you know?" Quintus inquired, his voice now raised. "Why would you spend your days in misery only to learn in your death it was for nothing?"

Adir found his voice growing stronger and he spoke firmly with Quintus. "We'll always doubt, and Satan will make sure of that, but you have to remember the moments when you didn't doubt. You have to remember the moments when you felt God."

Quintus laughed aloud. "You will die now Adir, and when you finally do, you will realize you are wrong. Nobody can beat death. It is everyone's destiny."

"Christ beat death."

"THAT IS A LIE!" roared Quintus in rage. He thrust the hot metal into Adir's chest painfully. It quickly burnt through the tunic in a stream of gray smoke and reached the skin with a horrid sizzling sound. His muscles instantly went rigid at the shock of the burn, sending him into more fits of pain. "Christ's deluded followers stole His body, claiming it was a miracle of their imaginary God."

"Quintus," Adir said, with a sincerity that surprised even him, "I hope you find God one day."

Quintus spat down at Adir and applied the glowing metal to the now exposed skin on his chest, this time holding it even longer. "You will die," said Quintus as he kicked again and again at Adir. "No healer can save you now, no God." Adir felt blood rush over his agonized body as his wounds were opened again. He didn't know when Quintus stopped, but after a long while he was left alone to die. But he forced his mind to look to his Lord, as hard as it was, for it was the only thing left to do. He wanted to stop, to give up, to finally let himself die, but he cast up his heart to Christ, seeking anything from Him. And suddenly, an impulse beyond reason or explanation drove him to sing. And he praised Him with all of his being, pouring out his soul to the Creator and to Christ. He felt the presence of the Holy Spirit around him, comforting him. He felt no more pain. He no longer felt death closing in on him. He racked his memory for any words, any thoughts, anything at all to praise Christ. Time melted away, and he was unaware of anything except a calm, restful peace and darkness around him. He did not die. He did not pass out. He slept.

THE VICTOR PART II

CHAPTER SEVEN
THE NEXT DAY

Adir's eyes opened in a flash as he sat abruptly upright. His stiff muscles vehemently protested the movement and jagged lines of fiery pain traced their way across his body. He lowered his head, enduring the wave of aching, but was surprised at the vast improvement in his condition overnight. Under normal circumstances, it would have taken a healer more than two weeks to get him this far. He looked down at his body, still clothed in the torn red tunic. The gaps in the fabric revealed gruesome wounds, but they had obviously healed.

Just then, the door to his cell was opened and Fulvianus stepped in. In one hand the bestiarius held a roll of white gauze, and in his other a clay pot which Adir guessed held a medicinal substance. He opened his mouth slightly to speak, but Fulvianus addressed him first. "You saved my life, and now I will save yours." He crouched to his knees and dipped his fingers in the pot, coating them in a salve. He busied himself applying it to Adir's wounds before wrapping the gauze around it. "I wish it were someone more trained for the job," he muttered. "They could do more than this. But the

89

salve is good. They use it on gladiators, I'm sure you know, but it will help fight infection and heal it quicker. For now, this is all I can do."

After a while, Fulvianus asked him, "Why did you do it?" In response to Adir's quizzical glance, he continued. "Why did you save me?"

"I have experienced God's mercy many times, and I knew I could not serve a God of His compassion while letting you die. I wish I could have saved the other Christians, but…"

Fulvianus nodded, and as he finished with the bandages, he left without another word. Adir awkwardly shuffled to the other side of the cell and slouched against the wall. He lifted his head toward the sky and smiled ever so briefly. He was serving the Lord. He bowed his head and prayed fervently. He prayed for healing; for safety; for deliverance from Rome. When he looked up again, Quintus was standing outside of his cell, though peculiarly he was paying no attention to Adir. His attention was fixed on a young boy standing in the hallway. "You say you bring me news of this slave's master?" Quintus inquired, gesturing to Adir.

"His master is dead," the boy stated blatantly. "And his only named successor has fled to the wilderness."

Adir's mind reeled. Semerkhet dead? Diomed running away? Only in horrible fantasies had he ever considered that Semerkhet might one day die.

THE VICTOR PART II

The cruel man had seemed immortal, invulnerable. He was grimly satisfied with the death, feeling some of the intense sentiment that had grown in him since early adolescence release. But he swept the wicked thought from his mind, forcing himself instead into cold indifference. Quintus waved the messenger away and turned to Adir with a twisted smirk on his face. "You're mine now." Adir's heart panged, and his throat constricted. *No.* He felt frustration inside of him, more than ever before, but not only at Quintus. At God. He had begged Him for anything to bring him out of this, and this was what he got. What happened to the miracles? He had certainly believed another one was coming. And now he was only pulled deeper into his troubles. Quintus left once more, chuckling to himself.

Adir was startled when he found Fulvianus opening his cell door a few hours later. The sun was just beginning to sink down to the western part of the sky. Fulvianus tossed some bread and salted pork onto Adir's lap, and he ate quickly. It felt good to have food in his stomach again.

"Who is he?" Fulvianus asked.

"What?" inquired Adir, slightly exasperated.

"Jesus. I need to know more about him."

Adir thought for a moment to gather himself before speaking to the bestiarius. "He was a miracle. Everywhere He went, the blind could see, the lame could walk. He was the Son of God, the true Messiah. He loved all those who scorned him. He adored all those who despised Him. He healed nations and saved countless people from the wickedness that mars God's once glorious Earth. But He was ridiculed. Mocked. Murdered."

"Rome killed Him," muttered Fulvianus.

"But even death could not win out over Him. Three days He took on the penalties for every person's sin in Hell. And then, He emerged from the grave. Victorious."

Fulvianus looked up, his sagging face a mixture of emotions.

Adir was smiling broadly, elated as he spoke the Good News. "He wants you to dwell with Him where He sits at the right hand of God. Salvation is there, waiting for you."

"How do I know?" Fulvianus asked.

"You don't really, but I, like so many others, am sure of it. You can be, too."

"How?"

"Pray, open yourself up to God, and for just a few minutes, believe. Pray whenever you can, and when you feel His presence, you will know. And you have to keep that in mind when trials come your way."

Just as before, Fulvianus hastened away with a startling lack of speech.

THE VICTOR PART II

Adir sat contemplating his short conversation with Fulvianus for several minutes until Quintus entered his cell. "All you people must really like me, to visit this much," he said, to elicit a snarl from Quintus. "But it's getting bothersome. I can't seem to get any rest." Quintus scowled and spat down at Adir. Struggling, Adir forced his tremulous limbs to support him, and for the first time in nearly twenty hours, he stood. His limbs were weak and any inkling of his strength, which had won him repute and saved his life many times as a gladiator, was gone or drowned under the pain that wrapped around him. He would not allow any of the pain to show on his face, any more than his taut muscles already betrayed, and he met Quintus' disdainful, seemingly defendant gaze with a defiant stare of his own.

"You are my slave, boy." Adir noticed that the Roman was balling his hand into a fist, but he did not alert his counterpart of the knowledge, remaining stoic even as he faced Quintus' rage. "I could end your life in an instant." Quintus paused and let the grim truth sink in. "I've been killing people in your deluded cult for years, and trust me, when I was done, they never believed any more. I crushed the faith out of them just as I crushed the life out of them. And when they finally deserted their precious Christ, then they die."

Quintus spun on his heels and left Adir. Horror was welling inside of him. He lowered himself to the floor and laid back again.

On the other side of the arena underbelly, Fulvianus trotted down the corridor to his quarters. Once inside, he threw himself onto the rough pallet. He was shaking in fear. He may be bestiarius, but he was a slave like any other. His lions had failed, and now he was visiting the one who had caused the mishap and embarrassed their arena. If his master discovered his visits, he would be killed.

Fulvianus closed his eyes, not to sleep, but to pray. He had never done so in his life. His mind was churning, but through it all, he was able to focus on the God he had persecuted for so long. His eyes were closed for many minutes, and when he opened them again, he believed. There was no doubt, no uncertainty. But he could feel somewhere deep inside of him, still uneasy with the faith. At first he thought it was his own instinct, but then he realized it was not him at all. It was the evil one. He had heard about him many times from the Christians, and this enemy seemed to be fighting hard. Everything around him and soon nearly everything inside of him, too, was forcing him away from the brief flare of faith. Surely, he would have been overpowered if he had not clung to the faith with all his will. He knew it could save him. He steeled his nerves, and allowed himself to trust in Jesus, and in God. In a moment the evil one was gone.

He smiled, his victorious faith strengthening him. He was ecstatic, silently worshipping his Lord, until he heard the bolt of a heavy door being pulled back. He looked up and saw two Praetorian soldiers shuffling into his room. The Roman soldiers, in direct service to the Emperor, the elite legionnaires, had been swarming the arena since Emperor Titus had sent them to deal with Adir and appointed Quintus their officer. Fear lurched into Fulvianus' mind, but his hope in Christ still filled him with strength.

Quintus was ushering Adir out of his cell and roughly pushing him down the hallway. "You will see your friend's death," Quintus stated menacingly. Adir begrudgingly lifted his gaze to the barred opening that provided a view of the arena when Quintus allowed him to stop. Fulvianus was led into the arena by two Praetorians. Suddenly, he looked at Adir, filling the latter with guilt. Adir knew he had caused this. Much to his surprise, though Fulvianus did not cast an accusatory glance. It was loving. Hopeful. The hints of fear curling around the bestiarius' demeanor disappeared under his inexplicable glee.

"I believe," Fulvianus shouted joyfully. "I believe!"

One Praetorian forced Fulvianus to his knees as the other drew his sword. The executioner extended his arm so that the cool blade touched Fulvianus' neck. He would not kill him honorably, like a warrior, with a sword down his back. They wanted to disgrace his failure. They wanted to please the crowd. The Praetorian drew his arm back before hacking down again. Adir averted his eyes quickly as the blade met Fulvianus' neck. Adir struggled not to retch as his friend's blood exploded across the arena. Fulvianus' head dropped to the ground and Adir was in tears before he could stop himself. "You're monsters," Adir spat at Quintus.

The Roman seemed unabated and replied to Adir in his usual leer. "You will die like him soon, but first your faith will fail." Quintus smiled grimly, as if his success was ensured. "You. Will. Succumb." Each word was forced out as a blatant, almost taunting statement. Adir stepped away, shocked and saddened by Fulvianus' death.

Quintus grasped Adir's shoulder and led him away. As they walked down the hallway, Adir saw a large, soft, round man approaching them. His stature, fine dress, and disgusted attitude to his surroundings betrayed his pampered life and riches. When he came to Quintus, he spoke quite loudly. "This place stinks of death. It's much more attractive when you're up there, in the spectator seats."

"Yes," Quintus nodded in agreement.

The stranger then stared appraisingly at Adir. "So this, Quintus, is your new slave, the Christian?" The fat man muttered the last words as if they were poison.

"Indeed, Decimus." Quintus shoved Adir closer to Decimus, who took him in his own grasp.

"Optimus would like to see him."

CHAPTER EIGHT

Decimus led Adir among the maze of wretched cells, followed by Quintus, until they began to ascend to a gate. Quintus stepped up before his superior and opened it for him. Decimus nodded appreciatively as he passed Quintus, who closed the gate again. They were under the spectator seats, and dusty rafters and scaffolding crowded the area. A few stairways led upward, to seats, or aside, to a quick exit. This arena had been an imitation of the coliseum, built only a few years after construction had started on the Circus Maximus, which had been completed just two years before. It contained the same engineering and prodigious design, though it was smaller. Even when it seated thousands of people, it could be evacuated in minutes in case of emergency. Any sunlight shining through gaps in the planks blinded Adir, after so long in the darkness of the arena underbelly. They walked swiftly to an exit, and Quintus swung open a door and they emerged into the streets of Rome.

Decimus handed Adir back over to Quintus and walked ahead of them among the throngs of people of every nationality. The stench hardly registered to Adir after his time in the decaying death-filled arena. Adir tried to exclude the crowd around him from his thoughts, but this was to no avail. Soon, he began to wonder who this Optimus was. He noticed Decimus was now thankfully turning away from the main road, and the largest crowd.

They were now journeying through the alleyways, populated by beggars soaking in their own despair and filth. Adir had been one of them once, though not in Rome, and he did not look kindly upon the memory. Presently, they reached a small home. It was identical to the others, in fact rather insignificant save the two horses and a mule, tended to by a young boy, standing in the small yard. The boy held the beast's tethers, and Decimus held out his hand for it. "Give it here, slave," he spat. The boy handed over his ropes and was waved away. Adir was sympathetic to his plight, and strove to denounce the fat Roman for his cruelty, obvious from the bruises that marred his slave boy's limbs.

Decimus pulled out a long, unattached rope from the others and seemed to be smiling to himself as he, with the help of Quintus, secured the rope around Adir's wrists. It was by now a familiar feeling to him. There was still ten feet of rope extending ahead, and Quintus took up the free end. The two Romans mounted the horses, and Quintus yanked violently on Adir's rope. "On the mule."

Adir struggled not to chuckle, mounting the remaining animal as he saw Decimus nearly fall from his horse. His enormous girth made it unnaturally difficult for him to maneuver in the saddle.

The entourage set off at a canter, continuing through the paved streets with a rhythmic clatter of hooves. Adir's head sank in as he thought of Fulvianus' death, but he was heartened by the fact he had known Christ when he died. Adir then thought of his wounds. They were healing rapidly, and though he was in no good condition, another couple of weeks and he would be in good health. At least he could function well.

The horses and mule carried the three at a steady rate. They were silent as the animals trotted on. Seeing a wealthy, powerful man and a Praetorian officer riding together enticed the crowd to part, and their journey was undisrupted. Several minutes after they departed, Decimus spoke. "He's rather young, isn't he?" he commented.

"Yes," Quintus said. "As a gladiator, gamblers would bet against him because he was barely a man and they would always lose their money."

"How good of a fighter was he?"

"He never lost. They say he was the best in Egypt, and most say the best in the whole Empire."

"Bah!" cried Decimus. "He may be good, but the gladiators of Rome would crush him." Decimus looked appraisingly at him. "He may be able to fight again, for us in the arena."

"Never," Adir said forcefully.

"So he can speak, too. No matter. You will die soon, and I will be rid of you."

Quintus seemed disappointed, and slightly resentful that he had lost control of the situation to his superiors, and he spoke venomously. "He has an annoying habit of escaping situations like that." He cast a hateful glare in Adir's direction. Adir smirked, enraging the Praetorian.

"Well, you know Optimus will have something special planned. He takes everything over the top. I'm excited to see it."

Adir suppressed a groan. *So Optimus is just another person trying to kill me.*

Silence again dominated their progress. After a long while of riding, they reached one of Rome's gates. The soldiers on either side bowed to Quintus and Decimus and beckoned them through. Decimus smiled to Quintus. "Being the friend of a Praetorian officer has advantages."

"As does being the friend of a senator."

Adir was becoming ever more curious even as he became fearful. Quintus was an officer of high standing who could call to his aid the might of the Roman army and thousands upon thousands of men who would die for him in an instant. Decimus was a senator, a political figure that could sway the ambitions of the Emperor himself. Who could Optimus be?

After they emerged from the gate, they followed the crowded cobblestone for a while. Adir was startled at the crush of men, beasts, and vessels carrying shipments of all kinds. The ring of voices and clatter of hooves and wagon wheels against the pavement swelled around Adir. He cast his mind away from the crowd and gazed around, marveling at the rolling hills of Italia that surrounded Rome. Adir struggled to keep his thoroughly spent body from collapsing. His head sagged, and his bound arms fell to his lap, though settled from their place at regular intervals from a tug by Quintus. Adir's body swayed with the gait of his mount. For many minutes they trod on until Decimus, at the lead, turned them off of the road.

Their journey turned to the hills. They plodded on as the earth rose on all sides, before retracting and falling away as they ascended on a peak. As they reached the crest of a high hill, Adir surveyed the rippling terrain. The road carved a path through the hills, flowing into Rome with the other roads, like the pulsing veins of the great beast, the dark, looming city. Decimus paused on the hill, as if reflecting on where to go next. He nodded his head abruptly, apparently reaching a decision, and urged his steed on.

The entourage followed the senator until Adir looked up to suddenly see a breathtaking view of a vast estate and villa sprawling through the hills. Livestock swarmed the immense pastures and crops, swaying in the breeze downcast from the higher ground around it, blanketed scores of acres. In the center of it all, though, was the most imposing villa Adir had ever seen. It was at least the size of a small town, and of its dozen buildings each seemed more massive than the next, with towers and battlements that made the place look like a military fortress. This Optimus must be as rich as Emperor Titus himself, Adir reflected. A dirt path, surprisingly, led to the villa's main entrance, and judging from the path's appearance, it had not been constructed but formed solely by the passage of countless men and animals.

The three followed the way until they rose upon a hillock to face a huge gate in the wall. The thick, heavy wood was set with numerous iron bolts and stretched bands. In front of the wall stood several pillars, and in the alcove between each, there were placed elaborately carved and jewel-adorned statues. They depicted the gods of the Romans and the deities of many of the provinces they had conquered. Adir recognized the figures of the Egyptian gods, standing majestic and regal after the twelve Olympians. He knew them from Semerkhet's villa, where they had been forced to worship them. He gazed in disgust at the ten foot tall statue, half human and half animal. He knew only one God now, only one Lord.

Decimus dismounted and approached the gate. He lifted the hefty iron ring and let it fall against the wood with a palpable, resonating thud. He waited a few minutes after the tone had died away, and when nothing came, he rapped against the wood, hard, with his knuckles. Still nothing. He puffed with exasperation, and charging like a bull threw all his respectable weight into the huge door. A significant boom shivered in the air. Decimus stood back expectantly. Quintus awkwardly cleared his throat, apparently dismayed at his companion's behavior. All eyes were on the gate when it began to creak open. Out of the gap appeared the head of a young man about Adir's age.

"Have you come to see Master Optimus?" Decimus nodded in affirmation. "Senator Decimus I presume," the servant said, smiling and bowing with what Adir recognized as a forced expression. "And Quintus, the hero of our god Mars." The veteran bowed, alight with conspicuous self-adoration.

The servant braced his body against the gate, his face tightening with exertion and then falling with relief as the door swung forward on its hinges to grant the visitors passage. The servant stepped aside, beckoning them through. They followed his outstretched arms into a courtyard. It was plain, a hundred yards of earth baring short-cropped grass in patches throughout. The young attendant took the bridles of the three beasts, and Quintus and Adir dismounted. The servant led their steeds away to the east wall where they exited the yard.

A middle-aged woman was now coming towards them from a similar door on the opposite wall. When she reached them, she spoke simply, "Follow me, sirs." She set off briskly, and they followed her across the courtyard and into a small room filled with half a dozen servants, with a staircase and two doors leading off. Adir glanced into one doorway, recognizing it as the servant's quarters. It was a larger room than he would have guessed from the entrance.

His attention was taken from the room when Quintus jerked on his rope. They ascended the stairs. Adir now noticed the gray stone with which the interior was built. It was used ubiquitously throughout the villa, and it gave the place a dismal atmosphere. Fittingly, torches lined the walls in rusted metal brackets, though they were not lit for the sunlight streaming through the thin rectangular windows.

When they reached the top of the staircase, the woman turned aside to let them pass. "Master Optimus is through that door, sirs," she stated in a monotone. Decimus did not acknowledge her, but went to the door without hesitation. He swung it open to reveal a room similar to the one previous it, save luxurious furnishings and even more servants lined up on two walls. At the far end of the room a lavish chair, almost like a throne, stood prominently. In front of it was a table, littered with the remains of an extravagant meal, flanked by a blue sofa and a bed strewn with blankets and pillows. In the great chair lounged a man with the size of Decimus but the sinewy, muscular bulk that filled out Quintus' slightly smaller but obviously more nimble body. His features were imposing and his countenance was that of arrogance and supremacy. His skin was shaded a dark brown by exposure to a strong sun, much like Adir's. Optimus, for that was undoubtedly him, addressed Decimus. "Ah, my old friend, have you forgotten how to knock or announce yourself in any way?" He spoke with the ease and assurance granted only to those who had conquered the deep, winding paths of philosophy.

"You asked for me," Decimus said, seeming perplexed.

"I asked for the slave," Optimus corrected. "And now, great Quintus, you can relieve yourself of your watch over him. My servants will attend his safekeeping." Adir saw two slaves approaching, one from each side. One removed a dagger and slashed the rope binding him. Before he could move, though, an uncannily strong grip secured his forearm and clapped manacles around his wrists. The two servants took up the chains. He struggled against them until Quintus rounded on him, fist cocked back, ready to strike him down.

The slaves pulled back the chains until his arms were pulled tight, directly outward from his sides, almost at shoulder level. Then they bolted the chains to the floor. No matter how much Adir strained his strong arms, he was completely immobilized. He fixed a steely gaze on Optimus who smiled in return and he resigned himself to fixity.

Seeing that all this was concluded, Quintus inquired of Optimus a simple question. "What do you want with my slave?" Quintus' arrogance seeped into the comment, and he failed to address Optimus, their obvious superior, with any trace of respect, an action made all the more noticeable by Decimus' preceding reverence. Quintus' usual demeanor was present, that he was above all others. Adir looked up to the one he spoke to, who displayed similar sentiments, and noticed he was aggravated, yet struggling to remain composed among his guests. His lips were pursed to suppress a snarl and his eyes and nostrils flared in offense. So Quintus stood, awaiting whatever Optimus might throw at him with unsettling hospitality, while the latter pondered carefully his actions in response to the officer's lack of decorum.

Optimus evidently decided to ignore it. "Merely to speak with him for now," he said and turned from Quintus to Adir. "Call it a trial of sorts. That is the Roman custom, is it not?"

Adir spoke out to Optimus, knowing full well the consequences of a slave addressing a citizen out of turn, especially one of such prominence as this one. For reasons he could not well explain, he wanted to try this man's temper. "Who are you?" Adir questioned.

Optimus chuckled slightly. "You're entertaining." In a flash, the man's features returned to their usual stolid form as he continued to view Adir. "But do not push too far. I will not hesitate to send those who annoy me to the Styx." He cast a sidelong glance to Quintus at this threat, but it seemed that no one noticed.

"In answer to your question, I am the governor, or rather, king," he glowed with pride, "of many of the Empire's provinces in Africa and the Middle-East. And even the provinces that I do not govern are so influenced by me that I might as well rule them. All of the forces of the area, especially the military ones, are under my command. Even Quintus must bow to my will when he commands troops there. And in that region, my power is only just surpassed by that of the Emperor.

"You," he said to Adir, "have stirred up trouble in my provinces. You have become rather a nuisance to me so I am here in Rome to discuss the growing issue of Christianity that has only festered throughout Nero's valiant attempts to snuff it out. If all goes well, I will get to kill you. Well, as I think about it, I'm going to kill you anyway."

For the sake of defiance, Quintus burst out, "He's my slave!"

"And you are mine." Optimus was glowering.

"I am a free man." Quintus spoke indignantly.

"No. You have quite recently, I recall, pledged yourself to ten more years in service of the legions in addition to your original twenty-five. I am your commander, and you are my slave as much as these here." He gestured to the ones lined up on the wall. Quintus was grinding his teeth and Adir was surprised at the anger between them. The elusive feud was evolving before them. Decimus stood aside unnerved by the tension.

After a pause, Adir said, "If you want to speak to me, do it."

"Why do you follow the teachings of Jesus of Nazareth?"

Adir paused, sorting his next words, but soon abandoned that. He would just have to speak the truth of what he believed. Maybe he would live a few more minutes.

"Are you a scholar?"

"As much as I am a soldier or a politician."

"Do you know of the God of the Jews?"

"I spent a couple months in Jerusalem studying the Torah and the Hebrew laws," he lifted the corner of his mouth in contempt, "but I hardly believed any of it."

The captive stretched over the floor in the huge room of the dark fortress gathered his resolve and spoke in utter truth. "Jesus is the Son of that God, the one and only God."

"One can hardly make a case for His divinity," Optimus said reasonably. "He couldn't even get himself off of that cross. No Son of God would die as He did at the hands of Rome."

"He had to die, to take on all the heinous sins of mankind. He loves us so much, He paid the price for our sins. Upon Him came death and Hell, but he conquered them. He rose again." Tears were in Adir's eyes now. "He won, Optimus, and in the end He will win again."

Optimus scoffed, his face coiling in resentment. Adir lowered his head and in silent prayer he asked Jesus to grant him His guidance and the presence of His Spirit as He had promised His followers fifty years ago after His resurrection. The Spirit came, filling him with boundless exhilaration and comfort. "It's foolish to put your faith in the heretic. When you die, there will be no real assurance that the cause to which you have devoted your life has been anything more than a lie. You will venture into death, waiting for your precious Christ to give you the everlasting life that I can very nearly guarantee you doesn't exist. Do you really want to waste your life away for that? Why not make the best of your life; indulge in the pleasures the world offers you while you still have the chance."

These were the same notions battling inside Adir even now, trying to tear him away from his faith. Doubt was ever present, growing stronger in his mind and forcing him from Christ ever so slowly. Again, he dove into prayer, striving once more for the peace in knowing that God was there. He devoted all of himself to it, and he was rewarded. The Creator was there, and he worshipped Him. It was bliss. Doubts assailed him, but they were cast aside. If only, in all the trials and uncertainty that awaited him, he could remember this moment.

"You're wrong," he stated. There was no sting in his words, but there was power. The triumphant face that had been growing on Optimus fell before he hurriedly gathered himself up again.

"There's hardly enough proof," Optimus said with finality. "I won't believe it until I'm certain it's true."

"What more proof do you need?" inquired Adir, "than Christ Himself rising from the dead?" Optimus remained composed and was hardly swayed. Again, Adir asked a question. "Do you know the story of Moses, and the deliverance of the Israelites from Egypt?" Adir knew he could not discuss this topic for any length of time as his only knowledge of it came from the Jew who had first told him of Christ in Semerkhet's villa, and their conversations were brief. Optimus nodded in answer. "You must have thought the Israelites were fools as they wandered through the desert." Optimus became quizzical.

"Consider for a moment," Adir continued, "that this story is absolutely true, though you do not believe it. The Israelites had seen their God perform countless miracles. He had brought plagues upon the Egyptians; He had parted the Red Sea; He had brought manna from heaven to feed them; and now, as they travel, a column of clouds guides them by day, a pillar of fire by night. And still they had little faith in Him. Surely, you think them fools."

"Yes. Anyone could believe, even I, if He showed Himself like that."

"Then why do you not? Christ has risen! There are miracles all around you! Every breath you take is a miracle. Look at all of earth's wonders, look to the vast stars. Is it not all proof? Every aspect if Creation tells of its Creator. Nothing you can ever say or think can change that."

"I prefer philosophy and science," the governor said. "They can explain all of it and indeed far better than any religion."

"Then think back to the beginning, the very start of this world. No philosophy or science can explain that."

"I've heard enough, you ignorant worm."

"You brought me here so you could kill me for my beliefs. You fear them."

"No!" Optimus exclaimed. "I do not fear them, I despise them!"

Adir raised his own voice, speaking forcefully, yet he refrained from aggression. He knew Jesus had only ever loved all people, and he was intent on following His example still, despite the difficulty. "You do fear them, for somewhere within your twisted heart you know they're true. You know that your wickedness condemns you, so you choose not to believe. But you should! Oh, you should! We were made to worship. Find salvation in Jesus. Optimus, believe!"

With his first statement, Optimus was outraged, screaming to the extent of his voice. He shouted to his servants, but Adir, thrilled by the Holy Spirit did not hear or care. A servant advanced from one wall, a short, thick club in his hand. He strode up behind Adir and bludgeoned his back. Adir reeled from the unforeseen blow. His vision flitted across the room, before landing again on Optimus as he gasped for breath. He said, with great fervor, "There will come a day when everyone will bow to the Lord, when everyone will see the truth. There will come a day when you finally believe."

"No!" Optimus roared again, so furious that he leapt from his chair and tossed aside the table in front of it. "None will believe. This heresy will not survive. But Rome, and the world it has created, will. That is all there is anymore. That is the truth, the life, and the way." The last words he spat out slowly, a wretched smile creeping across his lips. It was a mockery of Christ's words. Adir silently raged. His jaw clenched till his whole head ached. Optimus strode up to Adir, spewing curses at Christ. "The dead fool you worship was a liar and a moron. You will face your death today, and your blasphemous Messiah will not be there, or anywhere. You will see nothing. And the faith you have held fast to will be for nothing. It will desert you."

Anger rose in Adir, coaxed by the burning strength the Holy Spirit filled him with. He strained against his chains and felt the metal stretching and the nails in the floor rending. In alarm, the servant behind Adir beat the captive in the head and back with his club. Adir felt the pain, and it welled inside of him with everything else. So much pain, and confusion, and fear, and rising above all anger. He could no longer contain it. It burst from him in mighty torrents, and the destructive force was formidable. In a second, both thick chains snapped and fell limp at his wrists.

He charged at Optimus, fist cocked back, ready to hit hard. Everyone in the room moved at once, Quintus drawing his sword and leaping in between the two, and all the servants jumping Adir at once. Suddenly, knowing it was for no good, Adir let the anger melt away. He stopped struggling and felt the servants toss him down onto the flagstone as he moved despondently away from Optimus. "Seize him!" Optimus yelled and acting at once on their master's commands, forced him onto his knees, hands pinned behind his back (igniting agony in his wounds) as one rammed a knee into his midriff. At a silent beckoning from Optimus, Adir was heaved back up and brought over to one of the doors at the side of the great room. It was swung open and Adir was tossed inside.

CHAPTER NINE

Adir first found his hands and knees had struck hard, rough wood. Next, in an instant, he became aware of the heat, intense and overwhelming, like nothing he had ever felt before. He looked around and his eyes were assaulted with savage brightness. Flames licked around the wood he was on, and it took him only a moment to realize what was happening, but longer to accept it. The wood on which he was positioned was a narrow bridge, spanning the room from door to door, and below it was a ten foot pit, piled with heaps of charred wood and oil-soaked cloth, burning violently. The fire raged in a massive inferno, swelling in the pit below him and flaring up around the bridge. He knew he would not last long in here. He heard Optimus' voice, yelling to him, but it was faint over the roar of the flames. "Denounce Christ, and you may yet live."

Adir rose slowly, overwhelmed by his predicament, when it only became worse. A huge, imposing man entered onto the bridge, holding the shaft of an eight-foot spear, whose broad metal head gleamed in the firelight. "I will not lose faith."

"Very well," Optimus replied.

THE VICTOR PART II

Adir drew his attention back to the fighting slave before him. Without hesitation or preamble, the fighter pulled level his spear and thrust it powerfully at Adir, who sidestepped and leaned away. His footing became precarious as he neared the edge of the bridge. Flame swelled around him, searing his skin and blackening his tunic. Adir scarcely managed to maintain balance long enough to find sure footing and sway back to the center of the bridge.

Just as quickly as the first time, the slave thrust again. Adir seized the shaft of the spear this time. The huge man pulled away, and Adir strained against him. In normal circumstances, he could have held his own against even absurdly strong opponents like this one, but in present condition, he was forced to yield ground quickly and his stance was all the while weakening. Adir's chest heaved, the thick smoke burning his lungs. Quite abruptly, Adir's opponent yanked the spear to the side, Adir with it. He released his grip as he was swung back to the fire. Adir twisted his body in the air, flinging himself away before he could be cast into the flames and certain death. He slammed down on the wood, gasping, thankful for his survival. Seeing his enemy had evaded the fire, the slave lowered the tip of his spear onto Adir's throat.

"End the scum's pathetic life," Optimus instructed his slave. Adir prepared for his life to fade into blackness amid the undulating inferno, and feeling the Holy Spirit again, he was somehow able to face it.

The slave looked intensely at Adir, and must have seen his fearlessness, his faith. The fighter was perplexed, and even amid that horrible place, he asked, "What inspires you to this?" Slowly, unsurely, he took the spear from Adir's neck.

Adir rose to his feet. In retrospect he would have found it grimly amusing how hilariously unfit their circumstance was for this. But none of that was important, and he spoke simply but powerfully. "Jesus. Eternity. Peace." The slave's uncertainty swelled, for he was unable to shake the truth in Adir's voice.

He backed away from Adir, unable to kill him, despite the harsh punishment to ensue from Optimus, who now exclaimed angrily, "Enough of this!" There was a brief lull in happenings until both doors were opened simultaneously. Adir was grabbed by his scorched tunic and yanked out of the infernal room. He was led across the room in which Optimus had been seated and through a series of halls. Finally, they came to a confluence of corridors.

From the left, the fighter was escorted by half a dozen servants, Decimus and Optimus. Quintus was close behind Adir and the servants leading him. Two servants, as instructed by Optimus, broke away from the group and led the fighter into a room. The servants were armed, and with Quintus closed around Adir. They all stood, waiting. Guilt for the doomed fighter plagued Adir through his confusion. Optimus entered the room, and he knew the courageous slave would not have good fortune. Muffled voices came from the closed door. Soon they were raised, and the conversation was heated. There was little else for an unnerving while. Then, a cry of agony and a body collapsing heavily onto the flagstone. Adir's throat constricted, his heart leapt, and his jaw went slack. When the door was opened again, the two servants were dragging the body of the dead slave hastily away. Everyone present was unsettled, Adir horrified, and the servants fearing for their own safety. Why would Optimus have killed a valuable slave, rather than disciplining him?

Optimus himself waited several moments before stepping out of the room. His brow was furrowed, and he took a deep breath, as if steeling himself. He turned to Quintus, stating firmly, "I would like to buy your slave."

Quintus was dumbfounded, not knowing how to respond. After a long pause, he replied. "I want him dead and humiliated. For the sake of Rome, I shall see his end. I will not hand him over to you."

"1500 sestertii."

Everyone was taken aback by the offer. "What do you want with him?"

ANDREW MEADE

"The same as you want, but I have the means to see it through."

"I could end it right now!" Quintus said, as if Optimus' statement had stung his pride. He drew from his belt a pugio, the dagger preferred by Roman soldiers. He put the blade to Adir's throat.

"Two thousand! Two thousand sestertii!"

Quintus paused for a second, pondering the small fortune offered to him.

"You can take him," he raised his hand to stay Optimus, "if you can have him dead in a week."

Optimus was reluctant to agree to any negotiations, but by some strange urging he complied. Quintus took the pugio away, grabbing Adir's arm and thrusting him over to Optimus. He was frustrated, and his countenance showed it. "Come, Decimus," he said forcefully and strode briskly away. The fat senator followed. Optimus did not speak to Adir.

"Take him to the slave quarters," he ordered to no slave in particular and walked idly away. The servants led him back through the villa until they descended the staircase and entered the slave quarters he had noticed before. There they left him, returning to their tasks.

He walked to the other side of the small room, furnished with about a dozen cots, on one of which he sat. This room must have been one of several slave barracks. He contemplated much, puzzling over the things that had happened. Guilt hung on his heart. He sat silently for several minutes, and then the door to the room was opened. A tall male servant entered, bearing a leather bag. "Optimus ordered me to treat your wounds," he informed Adir, speaking in apparent loathing of his master. From the bag he produced many medical effects. Several looked familiar to Adir from his time in the ludus, particularly the infirmary, but others were completely foreign. He removed his tunic, trying not to cringe as the movement of his arms and the disturbance of the coarse fabric elicited pain from him. The bandages that Fulvianus had applied were stripped away. The servant examined the worst of the wounds and applied the medicine generously. He set about doing his best to tend to all the injuries, grimly reminiscent of Fulvianus' efforts and concluded by bandaging him once again. He fetched from his bag now trousers and a tunic, of a light fabric, and boots, thin but heavy-duty, rather like moccasins. They were clean and untorn. The servant dutifully took the tunic that was in tatters and left.

Adir precariously outfitted himself in the clothing. The tunic was red, just as the one before it, and the pants were of a light gray, the boots a dark brown. He was alone for only a few seconds more when Optimus entered. Adir instinctively stepped away, and the governor's expression showed something very peculiar—shame. Adir remained motionless, waiting for him to talk. Optimus spoke cautiously.

"I should not have killed him." The statement took Adir by surprise. Optimus quickly continued to speak. "I don't know what you said to my slave, but it changed him greatly. I do not think he quite believed, but he was drawn to Christ. Watching it, it was so strange. There was a force at work. It terrified and infuriated me."

Adir couldn't help but smile. "I told him the truth."

Optimus shook his head, as if trying to wake from drowsiness.

"Do you believe?"

Optimus burst into laughter. "No. I don't think I could ever live by the rules of Christ or God. Things have changed, but I don't think I have. I will help you, yes, but do not think for a second that I will ever believe." Adir was astounded, thankful beyond words. "Work for me today, and tonight you can go free.'

"Quintus will be outraged."

"Bah! He can do nothing to me. And besides, in a few days I will be leaving for Egypt. I have a fabulous villa just outside of Alexandria."

Optimus stood to leave. "Go to the courtyard, and from there Antiochus will show you your post."

Adir followed Optimus out the door but turned away to the courtyard as he had been instructed. He passed through the open doorway and came into the huge space. Boys and girls alike, all salves, bustled around the bare expanse. One man, a bit older than the rest, and dressed in finer clothing, stood in the center. He addressed the slaves in quick succession, scribbling hastily with a stylus on a wax tablet he held. Adir timidly approached. Antiochus, for that was who Adir knew him to be, glanced at him appraisingly.

"Ah, the Christian slave." Antiochus looked back down at his tablet, unsuccessfully hiding his expression. Adir disgusted him. Adir did not know what to make of this, but immediately felt it best to ignore the matter.

Antiochus turned around and began to walk swiftly away. "Follow me!" he called. Adir did so rather half-heartedly. Looking around, he soon discovered that nearly everyone here treated him with hostility. Most of them cast a sideways glance and shrank noticeably away. They passed under the archway leading west and came out into the sprawling crop fields that covered much of Optimus' property. Adir was directed to an area of the fields milling with workers harvesting the ripe crop. Upon arrival at the worksite, he was given the necessary tool, a long, curved scythe, and told to join the work. He imitated their labors, and soon fell into the rhythm of the work. He toiled away under the hot sun for hours. He enjoyed the hard work, though it exhausted him. At first his wounds were an inconvenience, but he quickly found his way to move around them, and he was glad to find that soon they hardly impeded him at all. Sweat drenched his body. His muscles were sore. Yet he was thankful for the exertion. Water was passed around every couple hours or so, and it tasted wonderful against Adir's mouth. A little while after the sun had set and all traces of light fled from the sky, the slaves were ordered from the fields. Adir with many of the other slaves went to the slave quarters he had been in with Optimus before.

He found an empty cot and collapsed there after washing some of the dirt and sweat from his skin. He was anxious to escape, as Optimus had told him he would, but he was frustrated by his utter ignorance in the matter. He knew not his own role in it, and his stomach knotted with impatience. But he simply waited. In a few minutes, the rumbling snores of the other slaves filled the room, but he kept himself from sleep. He just laid there, his eyes fixed on a crack in the ceiling tiles. He lasted only a couple of hours before he fell into a deep, dreamless sleep.

Through a curtain of drowsiness, Adir saw the flickering light of a candle. A hand took his shoulder and shook him from sleep, though the man was apparently oblivious to Adir's wounds. Pain flung Adir into wakefulness. It was Optimus who stood there in the waxen light.

"Come, Adir," he whispered urgently. Adir rolled from the cot and slowly raised his stiff body. He refrained from a groan. Optimus was already moving swiftly through the door and Adir thusly followed. Rather than going to the courtyard, Optimus bustled on in the opposite direction. Adir could see little of their surroundings, for the candlelight penetrated only a few feet deep into the thick darkness. Even so, Optimus directed them without hesitation.

Optimus slowed as they evidently reached their destination. They stood before a window, just a square gap in the wall three feet across. Without question Adir pulled himself over the edge and dropped down onto the cold soft earth beyond. He turned to face Optimus through the opening as the latter spoke.

"I don't quite know why I'm telling you this, Adir, but I shall anyway. There will be more games in the arena you were in today. Many, in spectacular fashion, to compensate for the embarrassment you caused them. The other Christians will go early. Just after dawn. Pray for them, or whatever Christians do."

"I shall." Adir nodded, now concerned.

He turned to leave, but Optimus addressed him again. "You represent a significant investment of mine, not only financially. Try not to get yourself killed for as long as you can." With that, Optimus disappeared from the window.

Adir turned on his heel and trudged down a gentle slope. The moonlight just barely permeated the darkness, but it was enough to see by. He heard owls in the distance. A small animal scurried in the tall grass near his feet. In a few minutes he came to a stream. He leapt quickly over and continued his trek. He knew he was completely unprepared for whatever came ahead. He knew not where he was going. He rose over a hill and slumped against the gnarled trunk of a lone tree. He was lost.

All of this, everything, was for Christ. He bowed his head and screwed his eyes shut. In silent, incoherent prayer, he felt the Holy Spirit again. *Lord, show me what You want me to do. Show me how to serve You.* He faltered for a moment. *Lord, You are everything. I give myself to You. I am Yours. If You can use me, I beg You, do.* At that moment he knew he could never do anything but serve the Lord. And he knew what he must do. The realization was like a blow.

He looked up to the great city of Rome silhouetted against the sun that was just beginning to appear over the horizon. It was dawn. Throughout the city, the games of the arena would begin. Christians were being murdered, and among them the ones who had been in the cell with him a few days ago. His prayer of only moments ago seemed so weak. Fire burned in his body. It was as if two armies were waging war within him. His chest seemed to bear a terrible weight. Sobs broke through his countenance. He stood and sprinted away. His mind and body were in turmoil as if his very being was unraveling. A minute later he fell to his knees at the bank of a river, the Tiber.

Adir simply knelt there and wept. The evil in that city disgusted him beyond thought. He knew what awaited him. Yet he had to follow Christ. He tried to recite his prayer, but his mind and tongue were forced to a standstill. He brought all his thoughts to Christ then. His savior. "*Jesus. Jesus.*" He muttered the name again and again and prayed with all his heart. He found strength there.

Suddenly, his will was resolved. His whole life was in Christ now. He relied upon his savior like a child, though all childhood was gone from him now. Though his life in the ludus had earned him a right to manhood that most people did not possess, he had for so long seemed a boy even to himself. Now his life was set, and his faith was absolute.

The man glanced into the churning waters of the Tiber as a pack, soaking wet and strangely familiar to him washed up. He lifted it and a wooden sword fell out onto the sandy shore. Adir

ANDREW MEADE

hardly refrained from exclaiming gleefully. He plunged his hand into the pack and pulled out a single piece of folded parchment, miraculously dry. He slowly read Matthias' letter. He was jovial and encouraged. He could hardly grasp how the pack had gotten here from the southern Mediterranean. It had probably drifted up through the ocean currents and into the tributaries of the Tiber, finally washing up here. But he did not ponder this now. He put the letter back into the pack, slinging it onto his back. He took up the wooden sword, a rudis. It still showed the deep gashes from its previous use when he had escaped Araby on horseback, but it was otherwise unharmed and it would still be as useful as before. Then he remembered what Optimus had said. The Christians were being killed.

"Esther."

He would have to save his friend. And so, he would have to return to Rome, and to the arena.

THE VICTOR PART II

CHAPTER TEN

The thought had awakened an overpowering sense of urgency. He knew there was not much time. Presently he sprinted along the Tiber for a while, until, as the ground flattened somewhat, he heard the bedlam of the Appian Way. He turned from the river path and flew across the gently swaying grass. He had always been one of the fastest runners when they were training in the ludus. He raced up to the road in swift, long strides. The sight of him charging up was quite bizarre, and the traffic slowed, some people even scattering before him.

Thankfully unhindered, Adir slipped in to the city. Praetorians attempted unsuccessfully to stop him, taken by surprise. He dodged a club and danced away from a soldier who charged at him like an angry bull. The soldiers growled in outrage as he sprinted on. They gave chase for only a few yards, but abandoned their efforts finding that their heavy equipment hampered them.

Then many sensations bombarded Adir from the city, previously delayed by the flurry of action. Furious shouting sounded behind him and the stench of Rome nearly sent him retching. He detested being in the city, but he dispelled the thought. The winding streets and narrow, labyrinthine alleyways were difficult to navigate and he slowed his pace. Soon, though, he came across an area that bore familiarity. He had only been in Rome twice, but as he raced out onto this street, he was sure he recognized the buildings here. He trotted across the cobblestone street, among the huge crowd and traffic dominant throughout the avenue. The noise was immense, drowning his thoughts in the din of voices and the clatter of wagon wheels and hooves on flagstone.

Adir hurried through the streets, frantically trying to follow the path Quintus had led him on to the arena. Yet the throng of humans would hardly permit him to do that. Time lengthened, and he pushed on for quite a while. Minutes passed and his jog became a run. He shuffled through the crowd, leaving a wake of people frustrated and unsettled. Then he caught a flash of a looming concrete structure over the top of a quaint brick home. It was undoubtedly the arena.

His hopes renewed, Adir sprinted round a corner. A straight stretch of about a hundred yards led to the arena. Few people dotted the street, most in the vicinity having filtered into the arena for the games. Adir looked back and saw a glimpse of gilded helmets. The crowd was splitting, leaving Adir to face three angry Praetorian guards. They were charging him suddenly, tower shields in front

THE VICTOR PART II

and javelins held in arms cocked back and ready to launch the projectiles. Adir turned on his heels and ran, leaping strides flinging him across the distance in flashes of motion. In only a few short moments he had nearly cleared the expanse. It was empty. Any Romans lingering in the area had scattered into the allies, out of which now came two more soldiers. The first three were far behind, hopelessly slower than Adir in their cumbersome armor. But these two were desperately sprinting to intercept Adir, and he could not dodge their blockade. The two soldiers hoisted their shields and let fly the javelins. Adir leapt at the Romans and twisted in the air to avoid the missiles, missing them barely.

His foot struck a shield and he pivoted, swinging his body around as he, aided by his momentum, vaulted over the heads of the Romans. One soldier was knocked flat on his back by the force. Adir somersaulted and landed again fifteen away. The arena before him was surrounded by a ring of pillars that rose three stories, similar to Optimus'. He raced across the remaining distance and leapt up. The gate was locked, and he knew he had no chance with the other entrances in time. He slammed into a pillar, almost three yards from the ground. He wrapped his arm around the pillar and braced his feet on the stone. His wounds ached as they were forced roughly against the stone. Then, Adir slowly shuffled upward, gritting his teeth against the pain. He rose as quickly as he could manage, but it seemed too slow at the moment. He was faintly aware of the movements of the agitated soldiers below him. They had no chance of climbing in their armor, so they simply stayed below so that he could not come down.

Suddenly an object shattered against the pillar an inch from Adir's head, sounding the shriek of metal against stone. Small splinters of wood were flung out and Adir saw an arrowhead fall from the pillar where it had left a sizeable chip. He looked behind him and saw an archer had entered the street. He was surprised they would loose arrows at him, so close to hundreds of people in the arena.

Adir doubled his efforts, rushing up the pillar. His agility was hindered by his injuries, but he could still move quickly and precisely. Adir now reached a platform, a divide between the two levels of pillars. Another arrow was released. He heard the twang in the bowstring and threw his body aside with abandon. The arrow sprouted pristinely from the stone where his head would have been. He collided with the adjacent pillar and, getting only a precarious hold, immediately continued his climb. It took tremendous strength to maintain his position, for only the thin furrows on the masonry, or flutes, as the Greeks called them, provided a handhold on the pillar.

THE VICTOR PART II

Finally, the hasty climb came to an end. He launched himself over a wall, flying into the arena. Spectators screamed as he, thankfully, landed in an aisle between the seats. The same familiar adrenaline and utter faith in the mission God sent him on brought him up again and he sprinted between the seats. A few soldiers were in the audience, and they snapped into action, but it was of no use. He was too quickly nearing the center. He saw the circle of sand abruptly, taking in the details quickly.

A dozen Christians, clothed in the skin of animals, stood in the center, terrified. Two bears were attached to the arena walls by thick chains on either side of the Christians, their swatting paws just out of reach of their prey. Wolves roamed loose, circling and slowly approaching the Christians, but staying well away from the bears. On the other side, a huge rhino threw its weight against the three heavy chains that secured it to the wall within a ten foot distance. Behind the rhinoceros was a pile of weapons, the only faint hope of survival for any Christian who could reach them. It was a job for only the best gladiators, not these people. Perhaps that was the next event. Optimus had only been too right when he said they were struggling to compensate for his embarrassment.

Without thinking, Adir leapt over the low wall on the edge of the stands when he came to it, and was hurtling over the arena sand and plummeting the fifteen feet to the ground. At a high speed, he crashed into the back of one of the bears. He could feel the bones of the malnourished bear through the matted fur and scarred skin. He was stunned, but perhaps not as much as the bear. The beast lashed out furiously. Adir was tossed back into the chain pulled taut by the bear and flipped through the air before hitting the ground hard.

The wolves saw Adir land, and must have noticed how he was weakened for a moment by the impact. They came for him, ready to feast. The crowd was astir and the Christians were confused. The wolves trotted within reach of the bears, for their mind was set wholly on their prey, and the bear swatted one aside, screeching and yelping, with the swat of one powerful paw. The two remaining wolves hurried away from the dangerous beast and continued on to Adir. Adir came to his feet as the canines drew near, and held up his hand. He knew not why, but he felt the warmth of Christ in him and a powerful motivation silently informed him that he was in no danger.

Though he felt utterly ridiculous, Adir spoke to the snarling, hungry wolves. "In the name of the Lord, stop!" The wolves were totally still for a moment, their muscles tight under their hides. Then, in unison, the both lay down before him like well trained dogs.

Adir strode away from the wolves, who remained in unnerving fixity, and moved to the center with the Christians. Though the wolves were no longer a threat, the bears and rhino did not seem to have quieted. A bear abruptly broke free of its chains and soared through the air towards the Christians. "BE STILL!" Adir commanded them. Whining like pups, both bears retreated to the walls and stayed there.

An old lady in the audience, with a hunched back, gray stringy hair, and a disturbing lack of teeth in her swollen gums shook her short gray, gnarled cane furiously in the air spluttering the words, "Witchcraft! Witchcraft!" as her spittle showered the close vicinity.

Adir turned away and looked to the faces of the Christians who could yet become martyrs along with him. He saw Esther and smiled warmly. "God is with us," he told them. They nodded, muttering prayers, a few singing hymns in low tones.

Adir faced the rhino and approached carefully across the sun-scorched sand. He silently prayed to God, willing the animal to recognize the Lord as the others did and spare him a fight. The beast's nostrils flared. Its armor-like hide shook as its tremendously powerful muscles strained. It seemed to Adir to tower above him. Where the chains were nailed to the arena wall, jagged cracks were advancing outward. Adir edged around the rhino, now saying his frantic prayer aloud. The beast followed his movement, keeping its hulking body in front of him and his fiery eyes fixed on him.

Adir glanced at the pile of weapons behind the rhino, and as he saw the opening shrink, he went for it. He surged forward. The rhino reeled to face him, whipping around the chains and letting out a great noise as they met their limit. Dust was rising in a swirling cloud. He saw the horned head charging forward, lowered to the level of his midriff. He immediately leapt away, towards the weapons. His mind working tenfold, he registered that the weapons were in reach—but pain suddenly exploded in his leg and he was flung into the wall, now fully behind the rhino. It had turned to ram again, grinding him into a pulp against the wall, but was now tangled in the chains. Its eyes showed its boundless rage.

The rhino stood over the swords and daggers and spears on the ground that would have been his salvation. *No,* Adir told himself. God would be his salvation once more. Lifting his heart to Christ, he stood and faced the rhino. Just as the others had done, it submitted. It stepped slowly away from the weapons. Adir came to them and selected a strong, sturdy spear. The rhino seemed apprehensive.

"My plans have changed. I will help you," Adir said, examining the eerily tame animals in the arena. "I will not hurt you."

Adir came to a chain that bound the rhino. He broke a link, and repeated the process on the other chain. Then, spear reversed in his hand, he stepped over to the rhino and pulled the chains off its body. The rhinoceros nudged his hand affectionately and he smiled uncertainly.

Adir moved from the rhino back to the Christians. His body felt strange, thrilled beyond anything he had ever experienced before. When he looked to the crowd he saw that they were befuddled. Adir then heard commotion in the maze of corridors beneath the arena. He looked to a gate leading into the circle as many heavy footsteps were heard behind it. He saw a flash of shining metal and the gate was lifted. In full battle armor, fifteen Praetorian soldiers trotted out behind their tower shields. At their head was Quintus. The crowd roared, either thinking this was all a show or being certain that the soldiers would save them.

Adir panicked for a second, before he was suddenly quite calm. The wolves struck out first across the sand, blurring into whooping streaks as they leapt into the midst of the soldiers. Next were the bears, lumbering into the ranks followed closely by the rhino. The majority of the arena was now a mass of tumbling men and animals, glimpsed only in flurried motion. The wolves were cut down, one by Quintus, and Adir was struck by regret. One bear was caught in the hide by a sword, only after mauling several men, and any who could still handle their weapons took it down together. The other bear fought ferociously until it too inevitably fell.

The rhino, however, was slower to fall victim to the weapons. Its thick hide was nearly impossible to penetrate. It barreled through the shattered ranks, bowling down any standing and trampling the wounded into lifelessness. Soon, only one soldier remained, Quintus. The rhino rammed into his raised tower shield. It shattered as Quintus took the blow. He was flung onto his back before the stampeding rhinoceros, and quickly rolled aside, came to his knees and submerged the blade of his gladius in the soft underbelly of the rhino as it passed.

Adir burned with rage as the gargantuan beast toppled to the ground, dead, and Quintus, having freed his blood-soaked sword stood triumphantly over it. In the action, the Christians had hastened to the other side of the arena. There Adir located a gate and heaved against its bars. It swung open only three or four feet. A few at a time, the Christians dropped down and wriggled quickly under it. Lastly, Adir dropped under the gate that he remembered the Romans called "The Door of the Dead."

Again, Adir took the front and led them through the corridors, rather aimlessly. Only a few

THE VICTOR PART II

moments in, he could hear Quintus following. They quickened their pace. Then, miraculously, they followed a passage that led to a door. Quickly swinging it open and bursting through, Adir found himself exiting out of a side of the arena and onto the streets of Rome.

He slammed the door closed after the Christians had made it out and turned to them. He panicked for a moment as he saw the animal skins they were wearing, thinking they would never get through the city in that kind of attire, but he left it to the Lord. "We just have to get out of the city. There will be danger, but we have faith. God will be with us. Go now."

There was hesitation at first, but slowly the Christians scattered, knowing that Quintus would be coming. Then, only Esther remained with Adir. He turned to address her, but she spoke first.

"I will go with you."

"Very well."

CHAPTER ELEVEN
THREE DAYS LATER

The first day out of the arena, Adir and Esther had fled Rome and walked several miles into the Italian hills until finding shelter under a knob of rock. They had kept their distance the whole while, and Adir rarely spoke. The weight of God's plan for him was on his shoulders. The next day, travelling far and feeling hunger gnawing at their stomachs, they had scavenged food from the hills. Nuts, berries and a squirrel Adir had killed—cooked over a very small fire that was snuffed out quickly after the meat was roasted—sustained them for another day of arduous travelling.

Now, as the sun emerged over the horizon, Adir sat up from an area of gathered grass and other materials that made a bed somewhat comfortable. A couple of feet away, Esther still slept. Their shelter was tucked into a small grove of trees. Adir muttered angrily to himself for his stupidity. He had not the faintest idea of how to survive out here. He shifted uneasily. Bugs had nearly devoured them alive overnight. And they were exposed to any predator who decided to do just that.

Adir silently woke Esther. Slowly, she stirred.

"Hopefully just one more day and then we can rest for a while," Adir said encouragingly.

Of mutual consent they ate and spoke sparingly before setting off. Adir trudged down a hill ahead of Esther and reached the narrow stream that carved a path through the rolling earth. Adir knelt by it and lowered his head into the cool water. He let the cold blast rush across his face and opened his mouth to drink deeply. He hoped the water was clean. Adir raised his head and cast the water off of his shock of black hair. Esther was also drinking. He waited till she finished and stood.

"I say we follow this south to the sea," Adir stated. "From there, we keep south and get as far away from Rome as we can, even if we fall off of the world's edge."

Even as the words were spoken, Adir knew he could not follow his own plan. He could not run away. He had to serve the Lord, despite the hardships that lay before him. And as he looked at Esther he knew she felt the same conviction.

"Well, perhaps not that far, but we must get away from that accursed city. Quintus will be coming at us with all the power of Rome, more power than either of us have ever faced."

Esther was quiet for a moment, but then spoke with deep assurance. "We have the power of Christ. That cannot fail."

The conversation fell to matters of their immediate survival and in a few minutes they set off with a fairly clear path ahead of them. For now, Adir busied himself with covering all the ground they could. They travelled parallel to the stream all the while. Esther had promised Adir that she could, and would, always keep up, so he pushed it, sometimes keeping at a trot for an hour or so. They travelled for a few hours rigorously until they were nearly collapsing where they stood.

At noon they stopped and ate again, scrounging from the environment. Hardly surprising, but grimly delightful, they were both eating more out here than they had in the arena prison. Adir, when he was a prized gladiator, was fed and treated in some ways nearly as well as Semerkhet. But before a fight, Semerkhet hardened him with brutality. Though they ate enough to survive, the pitiful diet could not support their pace.

Nevertheless, Adir set off again soon after their small meal. The sun was descending behind the distant crown of hills when they settled into the great roots of a large tree. For the first time, Adir risked a fire for the night. Even the small fire he had made to cook the squirrel had worried him, for he knew that the Romans were hunting them. Yet Adir could not resist the warmth of the dancing flames and popping logs as he set about building the fire.

By the time the world fell into complete darkness, flames writhed before his eyes.

Adir offered to stay awake most of the night in case the Romans found them. He laid the rudis across his knees and examined the wooden blade. He smiled wryly as Esther chuckled.

The night passed uneventfully, and after the fire was stamped out early the next morning, the day bore extreme familiarity to the one before it. Then, in early evening, the two stumbled into a squat little town with no more than two dozen buildings in its perimeter.

As Adir and Esther trudged up the dirt path to the center of the town, residents stepped out of their homes to view the bedraggled figures. The women stayed at the doors of their houses while a few of the men approached the figures. A tall man with a huge gut and untrimmed hair and beard stepped up to Adir.

"Who are you?" he asked.

"Two weary travelers in need of food and shelter. I am Adir and this is Esther." He gestured to his companion.

"Why are you here?" the man asked, skeptic of these strangers.

Adir hesitated. "We run from Rome."

The man was quiet for a moment. "We here are no friends of Rome. We have old Etruscan roots. During the unification of Italia years ago much of our tribe and others were annihilated by the legions. But still, I must ask you, why do you run?"

Adir did not reply. He was beyond reluctant to give the answer. Then, Esther spoke. "We are Christians. The Romans persecuted us in the arena. Our God delivered us and we are distancing ourselves from the city and those who hope to pursue us."

The man was at first surprised that the girl had spoken out of turn. Adir almost smiled to himself. Esther would never care for that. Then, the man heard what she said. His lip curled back in a snarl and he lunged for Adir.

A shout came from a recessed side street and the man stopped. Another man trotted out to where Adir, Esther, and the angry resident stood. The townsman recoiled as he saw the newcomer. He stepped back as the second man shuffled in front of the Christians defensively. "Let me take them. They will not bother you."

The first man nodded, reluctant at first, but then he bobbed his head solemnly, his face a void of indifference. "Very well, Eli, but keep them away from the town.

Eli smiled, nodded, and took in his hands Adir and Esther's arms. He led them back through the street where he had made his appearance. The travelers were not about to refuse the hospitality of this strange man, but Adir was slightly apprehensive. He noticed Esther seemed troubled by their encounter with the villager, but also as if she pitied him and the others.

The three left the main part of the village and they were on the hillside again. Only crop fields and some farming huts were there.

A few minutes later they came upon a fairly sizeable hut with walls of mud brick and slate, thatched roof, and an unfittingly expensive looking door. Behind the hut in a fenced in area a small flock of sheep wandered aimlessly, grazing where their heads fell to the browning grass.

Eli smiled as they came upon it. "My home," he said. "Not much accommodations for you, but I'm sure you'll find it favorable to the wilderness."

Eli led them into his home. The furnishings were sparse, and it was quite a simple house, but the two companions were beyond thankful for the shelter. Eli and Esther sat on roughly hewn wooden chairs before a matching table, and Adir perched on a stool. In a corner a pallet of straw and animal skins made Eli's bed.

"Christians, eh?" Eli muttered in amusement.

Adir and Esther nodded.

"I must apologize for the villagers. They are defensive of their tribal gods. But I've made it okay here, and it's nice to be in the company of fellow believers."

ANDREW MEADE

At first, they were delightfully shocked that he was a Christian.

"How did you come to know Christ?" Esther asked gently. Eli smiled, eager to finally tell his story.

"I was a leper. I had already lost a few fingers when Peter came through the area in Judea where I lived, miles from any others, rejected by the society I had been raised in. Peter was a follower of the Christ, one of his first disciples, and when he came by, he told me of his teacher. I wouldn't have believed him, but he reached out his hand and touched my infected arm. He said, 'I heal you in the name of Jesus Christ.' I unwrapped the bandages on my arm, and the leprosy was gone! I was a whole person again! Peter left me soon after, but forever, unflinchingly, I will believe.

"And he gave me this."

Eli went to a small chest tucked to a side of the room and removed a dozen or so scrolls. He beamed at them for a moment, proud of his collection. He hurried back to the table and dropped the scrolls onto the rough surface.

"The letters passed between believers. Accounts of Jesus' life and the wisdom of those who followed him. And this," Eli picked up a particularly thick scroll, "Is a collection of the psalms of David. I copied it during a fellowship of believers in Jerusalem. Read of all of them, please."

Esther leaned forward and picked up a scroll. Her eyes began to trace the lines of text, her face glowing with fierce emotion. Adir could for a while not fathom what she felt, but soon he knew that it could be nothing but love, deep and roaring, for Christ. Adir began to read the psalms Eli had laid on the table. Songs of praise. He knew he had to follow the Lord. He had to return to danger, and the clutches of Rome's evil. He craved these words of prayer. He read them slowly, savoring the deep love of God woven into each phrase. The room seemed to melt away as he lifted his spirit to Christ.

When Adir lowered the scroll, Eli looked at him with a smile.

Adir returned it. "It seems to be exactly the thing I needed."

"The Lord always provides just that."

A few hours after sunset that night, Adir sat up against the wall with a few scrolls in his lap. A shaft of moonlight he had positioned them in illuminated them enough to read by. Eli was lying on his back on an animal skin with a blanket looking at the ceiling. They had each taken a skin from Eli's bed and made their own as best they could.

Eli looked up at Adir and smiled. A moment later, he stirred from his place and came to Adir's side.

"I know you are troubled by something," Eli spoke softly.

ANDREW MEADE

Adir hesitated before he replied. "I know what I am to do for Christ. I have promised myself to the Lord and now I know what awaits me. I love my God, but I will never have a moment of safety or rest if I follow Him. The world will hunt me, try to destroy me, but I have to follow God. I am to declare the truth." Adir lowered his head and took a shuddering breath. He jabbed a finger at a scroll in his lap. "I am 'to go and make disciples of all nations.' "

"As are we all," Eli said. "God has something for you. A future. In him you will have life and hope and love. You said you will never have a moment of safety and rest. If you follow God, he will guide you to safety; in prayer you will find rest."

The two spoke for a long while. Eli encouraged him and as they read the scrolls, Adir began to realize the hope in God.

"God will never leave you," Eli said. "You will always have Him. His strength will carry and defend you. The world will come against you, but what is that against the mighty God who created it all?"

Deep in the night, Eli went back to his bed and promptly fell asleep after praying. Adir put away the scrolls and lay down on his arrangement to sleep. He closed his eyes and lifted his heart in

THE VICTOR PART II

prayer. Sleep came quickly, even as he was praying, and for the night he was at peace.

The morning came, and as the three left their slumber, they chatted idly for a while. Eli brought his guests a meal of bread, cheese, and precious mutton. After the meal, there was a lapse in conversation. Then, Adir spoke resolutely.

"I am leaving alone."

Esther opened her mouth to protest.

"I must," Adir told her. "This is my journey. Make a life for yourself, safe from Rome, if you can, and if ever I can, I will come to see you. But for now, a journey lies ahead of me. Quite the adventure. And for Christ, I must travel to the ends of the Earth and face the wrath of nations. But like Eli said, what are they going to do to the God who protects me?"

"Where are you going?" Eli inquired.

"Well, I can reach the coast in a day or two. From there, I will turn to Graecia, travel along the Mediterranean, declaring the Good News."

All was quiet for a moment, and then they set about preparing for Adir's departure. Esther said she would stay with Eli for a time, then find her own way.

Finally, as Adir was about to leave, Eli stopped him. He placed in his hand a scroll, the psalms of David. "Take it," Eli told him. "Please. I pray it will strengthen you."

With that, Adir bid farewell and stepped out of the hut. He situated the pack on his back and strode down the hill, past Eli's sheep, and wound his way down between the fields. He had set off on a journey, his journey for Christ. It was time to keep his promises.

THE VICTOR PART II

CHAPTER TWELVE
THE COAST OF GRAECIA ONE
WEEK LATER

Adir trudged up the shore away from the docked ships. The people milling around the port and the clump of buildings around it paid him little mind. A path, paved in the more well-travelled sections, but otherwise a dirt track, led back a mile or so to a town nestled into a bend of a river's tributary, backed against a wide green plain.

Adir stole across the beach and onto the path to town. His stomach was churning, his brow hot. He was anxious of what he was about to do, and the time at sea had not helped matters. In minutes, Adir was within view of the town, and his nerves trembled as he saw the wide cobbled road that connected the Grecian town to a Roman outpost.

With considerable effort, Adir was able to steel his mind and continue into the town. As he made his way into the market and town square, in the center of the buildings, Adir, to his horror, spotted the glinting armor of legionnaires, outstanding among the people of the town. The soldiers surveyed them with shrewd eyes and grim faces. Adir could not help but notice the tension between the soldiers and the people. There was hatred, hardly suppressed, among the majority of the townsfolk. They did not want the Romans here. As Adir looked around to the destroyed, burnt homes and stains of blood on the streets, he was fairly certain that revolt and unrest had occurred here.

Spotting a congregation of soldiers under a pavilion talking loudly and uncaringly among the others, Adir shuffled through the crowd and crept upon it until he could hear the conversation. Half-dozen soldiers were gathered around one other. By his outfit, he was an officer. He was flanked by two other soldiers.

One of the admirers flocking around the war hero called out, "You chased down the pirates? What then, Valerius?"

The man, who must have been Valerius, puffed up his chest and replied, "We took them down. I boarded the pirate ship and took down a score myself. Their ship sank, but I had already jumped back onto the marine's ship by then. Reaching shore, I came here, the nearest outpost." The other soldiers nodded, satisfied by Valerius' tale of his adventures at sea.

Adir regarded a young man a few feet away from him, also listening to the conversation. He looked Grecian, except for his inexplicably sandy blonde hair. His muscles were well developed, and his flesh bore the scars of battle, and his eyes were of a depth beyond his age. He had seen war, almost certainly with the legions. The way he looked at Valerius was strange. Many emotions raged from the youth to the officer, predominant among them despondent rage.

Now, with a touch of melodrama, Valerius looked into the anticipant faces of those in the small crowd as he elaborated and glorified the details of his story. As the Roman's gaze would have swept past the young man, he ducked away from the pavilion. Tiring of the officer's narcissistic speech and intrigued by the blonde soldier, Adir surreptitiously followed him. As the one whom Adir deduced as an ex-legionnaire brushed past another person in the crowd, his tunic shifted to reveal a gladius, tucked out of sight. Judging by its chipped and scratched blade, it had seen recent use and had not yet been mended.

Adir followed the stranger into a less trafficked and dilapidated part of town. Adir continued after him into a side-alley, but at a casual pace, for there was only one more person, a rough looking beggar, in the street. Adir glanced around in mock nonchalance. As he looked back to the stranger, he was surprised to see he had assumed a position next to the beggar, leaned against a wet, moldy wall. They were conversing in quick, low tones. Adir felt a tugging in his soul as he looked at the beggar. He had set off to serve the Lord.

Adir caught snatches of Greek phrases. He saw the Roman pride that had lingered on the young man disappear as he took the place of a beggar. He barely glanced up as Adir knelt beside of him. Adir swung his pack down and laid it in front of them. The beggar shrank back slightly as he saw the hilt of the rudis, appearing to be a regular gladius. Adir chuckled and pulled up enough of the rudis for him to see its wooden blade. "Not real, see?" Adir asked stiltedly. He had once known enough Greek in the ludus to have nearly fluent conversations in it, but he noticed it was rusty.

When the beggar relaxed, Adir pulled out a hunk of bread, an apple, and a piece of salted pork. As he pulled away the thin paper that wrapped the meat, the recipient's face lit up. The mysterious soldier looked up too. Adir smiled as he handed over the food to the two.

The hungry men tore into the food ravenously, obviously famished. Then, the soldier paused. "Why?" he asked.

Adir beamed at them before replying heartily, "For Christ."

The soldier tensed and a look somewhere between pleasant surprise and fearful awe swallowed his whole demeanor. Before quite knowing what he was doing, Adir spoke to them again. "Christ has done more for me than I can tell you."

Adir and the beggar talked for a time, and then the soldier steered the topic back to faith. Adir was eager to tell them more, and when the conversation allowed, share his story. From his escape from the ludus to the home of Eli, Adir told them of it all, especially of what Christ had done. He told them of the Spirit, of prayer, of the warmth and strength of the Lord. The beggar was transfixed, while the soldier stared at the cobbled street, deep in thought. Adir spoke passionately, and when he fumblingly failed to relate a word in Greek, he spoke quickly in Latin.

Some people moving along the streets stopped to listen to Adir, some to laugh and mock, others for curiosity at his strong words.

Finally, Adir closed, but seamlessly melted into prayer. Most of the people walked away, exasperated.

"*Lord,*" Adir murmured, "*You are everything. You laid the world of man upon this earth, and I know the love and strength in You, and the hope in Your son Jesus. Jesus. Our Savior.*"

Adir let the street fall into silence, but kept his head bowed, his heart still crying out in praise. When he looked up, worry had covered the faces of the people standing around him. The officer he had seen before, Valerius, strode up to him, raging.

"YOU SHOULD KNOW THAT ROME DOES NOT TOLERATE THAT CULT!"

"Indeed she doesn't," Adir agreed, "but for all her power, and all that she's tried, she hasn't done too much to stop me!"

Valerius glanced around at the people in the alley and his eyes fell on the soldier. "Titus! You're a fugitive! You should have stayed with the legions. Now I'll take you with this silly Christian."

"I don't think you'll be taking either of them." A man from the crowd stepped between Valerius and his two targets. Many others followed. Valerius glared at Adir and Titus between their heads.

"I pray you will know Christ one day," Adir said and stepped away into another street. Titus had already disappeared. Valerius was left spluttering at the people. One of his subordinates arrived on the scene and was just as quickly ordered to send a runner to Quintus.

"Tell him we can resume the hunt."

Adir heard this and quickened his step.

Titus slipped away from Valerius as he faced off against the Christian, Adir. He had entered the lowest level of a ruined building and backed away to the far edge of the room he was in. He fell heavily to his knees. He was bewildered, perplexed. Christ kept penetrating into his life. It was in such turmoil that he strove for one second of peace.

Then, with a strange feeling that he could deny the inevitable no longer, he bowed his head.

"*Jesus,*" he prayed, racked with passion at the simple word. Strength coursed through him, lifting his spirit to the Lord. "*Jesus.*" He said it again. It was the name of his salvation. Every feeling of this was native, and like a surging wave, it came quickly, drowning out everything else and filling every part of him.

"*Jesus.*"

It was sudden. It came quickly. The Holy Spirit. Perhaps it was just a gust of wind, but Titus was worshipping. He believed. And praise poured from his lips.

Then, it was over. Titus shook his head, finding he was breathing heavily. He didn't know quite what had happened, but he knew nothing would ever be the same.

ANDREW MEADE

CHAPTER THIRTEEN
NINE DAYS LATER

Adir staggered into the small outcropping. Two boulders were leaned against each other, and a small hillock had accumulated over it, opened in the front. He had searched the landscape for a natural shelter since the light began to disappear from the sky, begrudgingly moving on but hoping for a rest overnight. Now, after what he guessed was more than an hour after the last gray light of dusk had gone over the horizon, he collapsed into the small alcove.

With a sigh of relief, he pulled his worn and flimsy boots off of his sore, aching feet. He stretched out his aching muscles and reclined on the cool stone, his searing muscles finally relaxing. More than a week of travelling had been grueling. But he kept pushing on, mile after mile, hour after hour, for he knew that the Romans were on the hunt. Even when he was sure he had lost them, he eventually hit flat ground where noise travelled and the wind carried the harsh voices of the Romans. It entirely terrified Adir to think that his pursuers were only a few miles behind him. Yet, in a distant way, he admired Quintus and his men. They had kept up with him, at times noticeably gaining ground, even though he at times travelled more than twice as fast as Roman soldiers on campaign.

After a few minutes propped against the stone, Adir leaned forward and pulled his pack in front of him. He plunged in his hand and rummaged around for his food. His heart sank. There was none left. Doggedly, slowly, he took inventory of what he had left. Matthias' letter and a scroll of the psalms. The rudis and a small flint dagger from Eli. With a puff of breath and lethargy, he sank back again.

Then, he had a thought. If he was to deny his hollow stomach the comfort of food, he was certainly not going to deny himself the comfort of a small fire. Without thought of the danger it might place him in, he soon had a small pile of bracken and kindling.

Taking his flint dagger, he struck it sharply against a metal clasp on his pack. After numerous more tries of this, a spark leapt into the kindling. Adir gingerly nurtured it into a small flame and with a minute or so of gentle labor, it crackled into a quaint little fire.

As the smoke escaped into the utterly dark sky he hoped that the wind whipping through the air and the deep black would leave the Romans oblivious. At least his natural shelter would hide the glow.

Adir found a comfortable position and lay in the warmth of the fire for a long while. To keep his restless mind busy, he took up a branch about as long as his arm and pulled out of his pack the seemingly flammable wrappings that Eli had packed the food in. He was able to fashion a crude torch. He planned to set out into the treacherous terrain around him a couple of hours before first light, and his torch would provide the light he needed before dawn.

As he sat, Adir suddenly heard a scuffling some yards away. He paid it little attention and turned back to his fire. But it came again, and he heard a man breathe sharply. He was alert now and trained his eyes on the area where it had come from in the blackness. He muttered angrily to himself. His eyes had adjusted to the firelight and now there was only void before him.

Then, he saw a blade dart out and fall back into the night. Its opaque metal length reflected the glare of Adir's blaze.

His heart beat quickly. He was up in a flash and it took him only a second to light the torch and hurl it, tumbling through the air, into the one who held the sword. The flaming end took his shoulder hard, illuminating his shocked face as he stumbled away from the painful attack. Sparks exploded from the impact and the sheer surprise of it all sent the target into a gratuitous leap backward, rolling when he landed on his back and falling into a disheveled heap where he landed at the bottom of the small incline.

Adir snatched up his rudis and sprinted out. Reaching the man, he leapt onto him. He pinned his arms back with his knees and levelled the wooden blade with his throat.

"Just stop," the man under Adir muttered. "I mean you no harm."

Adir's eyes were by now well adjusted to the night, and from what little wavering light reached him from the fire, he began to make out details. It was Titus, the mysterious young soldier from the Grecian town with a dangerous history with Valerius.

Recognizing the face, Adir took back the rudis. He stood and backed away. Titus made it to his feet and took up the smoldering torch. He replaced his sword in his belt and slowly massaged his shoulder where the tunic was charred. Adir noticed this. "I apologize," he said meekly.

"Don't. It's no wonder you're a little paranoid, being hunted and all."

"Why did you draw your sword?"

Titus pointed to a large snake a couple of feet away, cut in half.

"Food," Adir said, smiling.

Several minutes later, the two sat around Adir's small fire. Titus made a passing comment on Adir's wooden sword. Then, as Adir looked at the youth across the fire, his curiosity was aroused.

"I've told you my story," he said. "Now tell me yours."

Titus began uncertainly, but then fully recounted his journey. From Valerius' cataclysmic attack on the Jews to his escape from the pirates with Julia.

"Julia and I moved up through Graecia, and Julia kept saying there was a group of Christians in the area bearing good will toward her. So we went a couple of days out of our way and managed to follow rumors. The Christians are ... notorious. We found a helpful fellow who sent me and Julia to a little house. He said the Christians were going to meet there.

"About a dozen believers were gathered. We stayed as they read letters from Paul and other followers of Christ and worshipped. I prayed and knew I would have to continue alone. Christ would have another journey for me, and all I had to do was follow a little and he would set it at my feet. When you spoke to me, I knew I was to go with you. Our journeys for Christ will be together."

"So you've been following me?" Adir inquired.

Titus chuckled. "Yes, but not hunting you like the Romans. I'm not even a Roman citizen anymore. I'm a fugitive, and now I'll be associated with Christians. I mean no offense to you by that. Anyway, my life from before is lost."

Adir roasted the snake, and the two ate a small ration. Adir carefully wrapped the rest and tucked it away in his pack.

"We'll get a few hours of sleep and set off well before dawn. We'll be leaving Graecia and entering Asia Minor before the next day is out. "

Titus nodded. He was relieved to be travelling with Adir. His provisions were scarce and he thought they would stand a better chance against the Romans and starvation together.

Even with only thin bedrolls, the two were quickly asleep.

Adir woke with a start. His heart fell as he saw the horizon. Dawn was already breaking. Any exhaustion was gone from him as he heard rough, commanding voices echoing across the landscape. He scrambled across the cave-like formation to wake Titus. The teenager barely responded.

"We overslept and the Romans have found us," Adir whispered sharply in his ear.

Titus' limbs flailed comically as he threw himself into an upright position. Adir would have laughed in different circumstances.

Adir and Titus hastily slid on their boots, kicked out the remains of the fire, crammed their bedrolls into the pack, and leapt out of their shelter.

Adir had given Titus the pack, and as they sprinted across the Greek countryside, he breathlessly spoke to him.

"Go into the hills. Find a place to hide from the Romans. I'll lead them away for a few miles then slip back and find you."

Titus agreed, unwilling to waste their time doing otherwise. Adir pulled the rudis out of the pack, not even thinking to get Titus' gladius instead, but he trusted the wooden sword. Titus disappeared into rough, hilly terrain littered with massive boulders.

Adir stayed back and turned to the Romans. He swung the rudis at his side, testing its balance. He trotted a little farther then turned away from the hills entirely. He could have slowed them in that terrain, but that was not what he wanted to do. In the hills, he and Titus would soon be killed. He prayed silently and fervently. His faith gave him courage to face the soldiers coming in.

He saw about twenty or thirty of them. At their head he saw one he recognized as Quintus, and beside him a figure who must have been Valerius. Then, Quintus spotted him. The soldier sprinted forward. Adir's body seemed drained of energy as soon as he saw the terrifying warrior charging forward, his immensely powerful, battle-scarred legs throwing forward his fearsome, huge body with great speed. Adir marveled at how he could run so

THE VICTOR PART II

quickly in full battle armor with a shield and weapons. Valerius and the soldiers were struggling to run at their fastest, and still were not keeping up.

Adir felt adrenaline, instinct, and everything he had ever been taught take control, and he was running, too. He flew down an embankment, only touching the ground every three yards to kick off again, heaving himself down the hill. As the ground levelled, he fell into an all-out sprint, pulling up his head and pumping his legs as fast as he could. His feet buried themselves in the soil with each step before he launched himself off again over the swaying grass. He must have run for a full five minutes, driven on past the extent of his gasping, crackling lungs by the thought of Quintus close behind him.

He saw up ahead an irrigation canal and braced for the leap. His body sailed over the space and he landed firmly on the other side, rolling as his feet dug into the soft soil and swung his body to the ground. He seamlessly came back to his feet and continued. He was in farmland now. Only an instant later he heard Quintus' armor rattle as he made the same jump.

Quintus was too close. Adir turned from the crop field and stole across the expanse into the more rocky terrain. He dodged around the landscape mutilated by thousands of years of erosion and slipped behind an immense boulder. Quintus lumbered on behind Adir and stopped when his prey evaded him. Adir stifled his heavy breathing. His shock of black hair, usually falling to his brow, was plastered to his head with perspiration. He flattened against the rock and felt his wildly beating heart thump against his ribs.

Quintus was only a couple of yards away. Adir heard him unsheathe his short sword. He was growling and muttering to himself.

There was a rush of air. Adir had not even caught sight of the blade except in a silvery flash before instinct drove him away from the boulder. Adir dove to the ground and rolled away as Quintus' gladius shrieked against the stone. Adir had missed death by a fraction of an inch. Quintus cursed loudly and lunged for Adir, swinging his sword again.

Adir launched away, into another rock and came back to his feet in time to dodge another attack. When Quintus thrust again, he batted the sword away with his rudis. Adir flung himself onto the rock and rolled down a hillock onto the lip of a dike.

Quintus followed after him, bounding down the incline. Adir shifted and fell into the deep furrow in the earth. Quintus jumped into the ditch, but Adir was already running again. The two raced along the narrow path. The walls of the trench pressed in on Adir's shoulders as he ran. He could hear Quintus having more trouble behind him, and yet he was still gaining. In only an instant he would be close enough to bury the gladius in his back.

Sensing the threat, Adir acted in a blur to avoid it. He jumped up, kicked off from one side and swung haplessly over the other side. He sprinted into the open and a dozen paces away heard a grumble of commotion. Valerius and the other soldiers were arriving from a shortcut. Most had shed their armor. The punishment for that would be less than for falling behind.

Valerius saw Adir and directed his men to charge their prey. Adir ran to a mound of dirt. Running up one side, he leapt off the other and cleared the heads of a few of the soldiers before slamming his feet firmly into another's chest, knocking them both back. Adir twisted his body as he was flung away so that he tumbled clear of the other soldiers when he landed with a soft thud.

The man Adir had struck bowled over the tight knot of soldiers behind him.

Then, Adir was once again flying across the countryside. He saw a barn. Without much thought, he decided to enter it. As he came upon it he swung open the heavy door and trotted inside. The dusty, spacious interior was dimly lit by thick shafts of sunlight that fell in between the weathered planks. A row of stalls was to one side, and in a corner a mass of hay. It was sweltering inside. He was exhausted and breathing heavily when he slumped down. He would be away from the Romans only a few moments in here.

Then, he heard them come. Quintus was ordering them to surround the barn while he sent a few men inside. Adir swung the heavy latch over the door and backed away. It shuddered as the strong men threw their weight against it.

Adir knew it could not hold for long. As it creaked and bent under the strain, he moved to the other side of the barn. Boards splintered and fell heavily onto the hard-packed earth, filling the air with a thick plume of dust. The soldiers burst in and the barn was at once filled with half a dozen men charging after Adir. Four brandished their short swords, the other two ready with their javelins. Adir leapt aside into a stall. The Romans pounded down to that side of the barn and formed a rough line in front of the stalls. One soldier would boisterously kick one open and the others would wait, ready to engage their target either when they cornered him or when he decided to face them. Adir's heart thrilled as they approached. Then, the wooden wall next to him was racked powerfully as the stall directly adjacent was searched.

Then, the stall's small door, swaying gently on rusty hinges, was sent flying into Adir as the soldier found his prey and barreled down the door. Adir tossed aside the dislodged door and dropped to the ground as a gladius rent the air. Chips of aged, tough wood flew as the gladius collided with the walls inside the cramped stall, and that saved Adir's life. Adir wrapped his fingers around the bottom of the wall and slid his body quickly through the gap between it and the ground just in time to avoid another sword thrust that pinned the blade only inches from Adir's head.

The Romans were crowding around the barn as Adir rolled back to his feet in the open interior of the barn. The soldiers wheeled around and ran after him. Adir lunged at them as they came, swinging down the rudis from above his head in a quick, snapping motion. The soldier blocked the strike from the wooden sword but Adir stepped up to him while his sword arm was still stunned and jammed down the pommel of his sword into the young Roman's arm where the armor did not reach. He then brought the wooden blade across the man's face, and as he winced and recoiled, he kicked him heavily to the ground.

It took Adir only seconds to dispatch the man and the next approached more warily, sword tip levelled with his heart. The two stepped forward and exchanged quick blows, but the soldier was trained for battle, not swordplay, and Adir flicked his wrist and with ease slammed his rudis into the back of the man's knee, and with an offhanded shove, the Roman flopped onto his back in the dirt.

Quintus shouted from the outside for the soldiers to hurry their work. The four left formed together as they approached Adir this time. It was about time, Adir observed wryly. He gave ground, buying time. The other two he had already fought joined the advance and he muttered in frustration. Adir did not know if he could fight six elite Roman soldiers at once without at least being wounded in the process. And, he didn't want to hurt them. His mind processed this quickly as he faced the Romans.

Then, they went for him. He saw the weapons speed through the air. He leapt nimbly aside and sprinted back to the stalls as the soldiers clambered after him. He jumped onto the wall of the stall and pulled himself up to perch precariously on the top. He stood, slowly, balancing with great care on the thin divide. He looked up into the rafters. With a puff of effort, he launched up from the wall and caught hold of the rafter closest to him. He swung up onto it and raised upright.

What sunlight filtered through the planks of the ceiling allowed Adir to see the other rafters. He steadied himself and shuffled forward. As he became more confident, he trotted along the beam. Then, he leapt to the next rafter, his arms swinging clumsily and dangerously over the wooden surface before he was able to find a sure hold and pull himself up again. Adir leapt from one beam to the other until he came to the main beam, wide enough for him to stand with no concern for balance. He looked down at the Romans. One stepped up and shouted to his comrades harshly. "Come on, get me up there!"

The men lifted the soldier and flung him up. With the boost, he was able to bound off the stall and catch hold of one of the rafters. He painstakingly pulled himself up and came to the main rafter with Adir.

The two lowered themselves into fighting stances and advanced on each other, muscles taut and ready to spring their bodies forward at any moment. The Roman flicked his wrist, swishing the gladius blade through the air. Adir knew the greatest advantage he had over the Roman was swiftness and agility.

Adir acted on the advantage, charging forward without the slightest hesitation and abruptly launched aside onto a support beam that branched up diagonally to the barn's vaulted roof. He rebounded off of the beam and landed just behind the Roman before he could turn and kicked him hard in the rear.

The Roman's balance faltered and he fell clumsily forward, before barely grabbing the rafter before his fall. But his weight was too much and his grip slipped. He plummeted to the hard-packed ground below with a soft thud and a wheezing moan. Quintus was heard shouting outside and then burst into the barn over the toppled doors and surveyed the scene quickly. He saw Adir in the rafters and snarled. He turned and shouted to some of the men outside. "Light it up!" he commanded. A man trotted into the barn with a torch and tossed the open flame into the pile of hay. The fire spread to a blaze in moments and thick smoke billowed up around Adir.

He coughed as his lungs filled with the vile gray material. His eyes watered and he struggled to see around him. Praying he did not step off of the rafters, he shuffled away from where the smoke was thickest. Finally, the billowing mass of smoke was no longer swirling around him and he was left to his own panicked thoughts. He saw through the gaps of the planking that other torches were being added to the base of the barn outside. Fires were springing up all around and the Romans had all left to join the others outside. The most massive inferno where the hay had been crawled up the wall and licked at the rafters. The dried wood and clumps of manure and straw were great fuels for the fire and it ferociously tore at the structure of the barn. Flame was coming closer to Adir and the heat prickled his skin. He looked frantically for a way to escape. The he looked up. The haze of smoke had obscured it, but Adir instantly saw the point of light. It was a man-sized hole, ringed by charred wood. The fire had eaten it away and then moved on. Knowing certain death awaited him if he stayed in the barn, he went for it. He made his way up the rafters, the smoke choking around him, until he was as close to the hole as he could get. It was ten feet away, and fire swelled in his path. Bracing his muscles for a quick release, he let them snap into action and he leapt. His wheeling limbs and squirming torso swept through the flames. His clothing was singed and the heat stung his skin, but he was not harmed. And as he hurtled from the blaze, he caught hold of the blackened wood around the opening.

He threw the rudis out onto the roof and hoisted himself up as well. He staggered away and sank down briefly next to the wooden sword, breathing heavily. The swelling fire roared and crackled beneath him.

Adir heaved himself to his feet again. The air was thick with the dark smoke that was streaming through the planks. Adir came to the edge of the roof and looked down at the line of Romans that had closed around the burning barn.

Valerius stepped out and began taunting him. Other Romans joined in and Adir could hear their jeers over the roar of the fire. Then Quintus silenced them and his booming voice broke over the flames.

"This day you die, Christian! The barn will topple in the fire and you will burn with it."

Adir could already feel the fiery structure weakening and knew it would soon crumble. Fear was welling in his heart.

But he forced the fear away. "I've survived things you never thought I would," he called back. "Do you really think this is going to end it? Is this all you're going to do? I thought Rome would do more than burn down a barn trying to kill me."

Quintus chuckled loudly and smirked to himself. He held high his gladius and shouted, "I'll kill you then!"

He charged forward and leapt at the wall. He punched the gladius through the roof and pulled himself up until he could grab the edge of the barn's roof. He removed the sword and swung himself up onto the roof. He stood to face Adir, sword levelled at his side.

Adir moved back to the peak of the slanting roof. Fire was bursting through the wood and the smoke was thicker than ever. Quintus followed in quick strides. Then, he lunged for Adir. Adir parried the blow and a quick exchange of dancing swords followed. Quintus' mastery was evident. Adir swirled, hacked and thrust furiously to keep Quintus at bay, but it was to no avail. Quintus was gaining the upper hand and forcing Adir to give ground. Quintus finally forced him to the end of the roof. Adir desperately tried to win back the ground he was losing far too quickly. The wooden sword

THE VICTOR PART II

landed on Quintus' upper arm and he reeled. Adir danced around to the other side of his foe, freeing himself from the threat of the edge.

But for an instant Adir's guard faltered and Quintus struck out savagely for the opening. Adir twisted away from the blade, but the sword caught his arm, laying open a six-inch gash on his forearm. Adir backed away quickly, clamping his free hand on his wounded sword arm as warm blood flowed freely. But there was no time to stem the flow. He passed his rudis to his left hand and prepared to face Quintus' onslaught again. He gritted his teeth against the deep, throbbing pain in his arm.

Quintus rushed him and threw his entire strength and weight into a downward arc. Adir held up the rudis to block and braced himself. The blow was devastating. Adir faltered and his arm almost gave way. Chips flew from the rudis. Adir was stepping away when Quintus swung his arm down again. This time Adir's strength failed as he blocked. His arm fell and he only narrowly avoided the sword. Quintus advanced again, striding forward, and with every step he hammered down. Adir held up his arm again and again, but with every block he weakened. Finally, Quintus went for the kill. He chopped down with one final, massive effort. Adir went to his knees on the barn's smoking roof, holding up both arms and praying that his fading strength would be enough to save him.

And the blow landed.

An awful crack sounded. Fragments of wood exploded out and two halves of the rudis fell to the barn's roof. Adir rolled away as his defense had fallen. The gladius continued on and buried itself in the barn's roof. Quintus leapt away from the sword and onto Adir. He pounded his fist into his gut and across his face. Quintus moved away from Adir and kicked his studded army sandal into his target's side. Pain was coursing through Adir's body. Quintus stepped away to retrieve his sword and Adir shuffled back. The fire was thickest in this area of the barn and flames were licking up around him. He came shakily to his feet and waited as Quintus slowly, deliberately, returned.

Suddenly, the barn trembled. The roof sagged and planks cracked. The flames crackled even more aggressively and swelled up through the boards. Huge noises came from below as massive sections of the barn collapsed into the inferno. Explosions of swirling fire replaced the dropping roof. Adir lost sight of Quintus in the chaos. He threw his arms up around his head, as if that would do anything.

The entire barn's foundation was giving way. The wood was splintering and collapsing. The roof at Adir's feet shuddered and jerked. He was thrown through the blaze. The blistering heat seared around him. He managed to land on some sort of structure and launched himself forward through the thick orange haze. He slammed against what he thought was a wall of the barn as it collapsed to the ground. He held fast to the wall. Chunks of wood and debris pelted him. Then, the wall landed with him hanging on and for a time his world was black.

When Adir came to, his body lay among the ruins of the barn. Blackened, smoldering wood was scattered around and on top of him. His muscles and bones ached, and he was slow to move. A large chunk of the wall pinned his right leg to the earth. His clothes were scorched and ash, dirt, sweat and blood left a layer of grime on him. Then he was aware of flame rising up the wood overtop his leg. He raised himself slowly, sweeping the rubble from his body, but his leg was still held below the burning wood. He struggled against it until finally he shifted free from under it. He looked dazedly at the mountain of smoking wood behind him where the majority of the barn had fallen. And his sluggish mind had a thought. *What if Quintus had not survived it?* Adir looked out at the line of Romans, or what was left of it. The explosive collapse of the barn had broken their formation, and they were unsettled by the thought of their hero, Quintus, lying dead among the rubble.

If ever there was a time to make a run for it, it was now. And so Adir did. He came to his feet and loped forward, clenching his teeth against his discomfort. As fast as he could manage, he ran past the confused Romans. They saw the figure flying from the ruined barn and scrambled after him, but they were now a dysfunctional unit and could not keep up. Valerius was in the far side of the barn and was too far away to run him down.

Then, the pile of rubble shifted, and Quintus pushed away the wood and emerged, rolling to the ground. He stood shakily and spotted Adir running. He still held the gladius, and he charged after Adir, hungry for his blood, eager to kill him. As he passed his men, he shouted, "Follow us into the hills. Scour them for him and his fugitive friend and make sure they can't escape."

Quintus turned back to Adir and sprinted after him once more. Adir saw the ragged, ash covered warrior hurtling after him, sword raised. His heart beat ever faster and he steered his path into the rocky foothills. Quintus disappeared behind the rippling terrain and Adir was left in suspense as he plunged into the treacherous expanse of rock and trenches gashed along the contour of the Earth. He raced away from Quintus, but his enemy was gaining, he knew. He vaulted over a boulder and caught a flash of movement over a hill to the left.

He urged himself to gain the high ground in case of Quintus' sudden appearance. He began laboring towards the other side of the slope he had ascended. His muscles were burning with the exertion.

THE VICTOR PART II

Then, he saw Quintus come. He bounded down the slope. Then, he leapt. He sailed through the air and slashed down at the Christian. Adir spun away from the blade as it hissed down at his head. Quintus cursed as he missed, but landed again and pushed back, not quite losing his momentum, and into Adir.

He tackled him headlong, and they both rolled down the hill. Adir blocked Quintus' sword arm as they fell, and though the blade jerked close to his face, he was unharmed.

Adir finally disconnected and scrambled away from Quintus, and though the Roman snatched at his feet as he ran, he received only flailing, yet efficient kicks from Adir. He dashed away again, followed closely by the remarkably tenacious Quintus. The chase continued around them, but Adir kept plowing into more treacherous area, forcing Quintus to check his speed, and if only by a little, it allowed Adir to retain the upper hand.

But the pace could not be kept for long. Adir was well conditioned, but the mad sprint was drawing on, and each heavy breath felt like flame as it raced down his parched throat and pierced his aching lungs. His limits were drawing near. Yet Quintus' fitness was adroit and he showed no signs of relenting.

Adir swerved his path to the side, and then he saw it. A massive field of crop, he did not know, or care, what it was, but it was taller than a man and swaying gently in the breeze. He sprinted down and plunged into the midst of the tall, shaking stalk. They crowded around him as he ran on. They smacked his body and face and swelled on all sides. He swept them apart in front of him and could feel them push back into place and settle again behind him. Quintus charged into the field behind him, furiously hacking away the stalks as he charged in Adir's wake.

Adir's only thoughts were of running, and of Quintus chasing him down. And then, he just stopped. He planted his feet and skidded to a halt, throwing up a spray of dirt. His chest ached, his throat burned, and his utterly taxed muscles trembled. He instinctively went to his knees. The stalks crowded around him, but he ignored it. He knew Quintus was chasing him, maybe even only a couple of yards away. He thought that perhaps he would charge up to him right now and strike him dead. But he found he did not really care and so bothered himself with the thought no longer.

He lowered his head, dripping with sweat and closed his eyes. Then, by an unseen but undoubtedly real and present force, he prayed.

He worshipped his Lord and he begged Him to help. He praised and pleaded freely. He prayed though by no spoken word, for he could find no words to speak of what he felt. So he prayed in the

THE VICTOR PART II

deepest, purest, truest belief. He felt the Spirit in him, swirling, gushing in his soul and all around him. It lifted his heart and he was begging to be left in His presence, in Christ's presence, in God's presence for just one more second.

Elation spilled from his heart and soul. And then, with one final rush of ecstasy and praise, it faded, leaving him grinning like a small child.

The dull thrumming ache had been cast from his muscles and bones. The pain of his exertions had been held at bay and he found a sudden energy and power. The Lord had given him what he needed to make it out alive. He stood and felt his mind sharpen. He could hear Quintus, tearing through the field a significant distance away. For a moment Adir plunged into his memory and finally managed to scrape up a sense of direction. The mad dash into the field and the minutes of confusion within it had left him clueless to his whereabouts, but he was nonetheless confident he knew where to go. He needed to make it into the hills, and on the scant hope that they might find each other in the sprawling wilderness, reunite with Titus.

And so into the hills he set off. There was no reason to avoid them now. He had to risk entrapment by the Romans. Knowing Quintus was moving in the other direction, he carried on at a trot. He soon emerged from the field and into the jagged terrain.

CHAPTER FOURTEEN

Titus had seen Adir disappear in the field almost five hours ago. From there, he had completely lost track of Adir. He thought, or at least hoped, that Adir would find his way back into the hills. Titus had skulked across the land all day, perilously avoiding the party of Romans sweeping the area for him.

He checked the position of the sun. A little past noon. He dropped down to a large rock and was content to sit in its shadow, on the cool ground, still damp with dew, for a while. He had been moving in the direction Adir had designated as the course for their travels, and it was hard going. He had eaten quite sparingly of the food in the pack, and his stomach felt hollow. His throat, too, was parched, for he had refrained from drinking too much of the water.

It was a grim thought for him to imagine the condition Adir must have been in without the rations in the pack. Titus' hopes were sinking, as he had seen no trace of Adir, but he was determined not to give up. With a sigh he rose, shifted the pack on his shoulders, and moved on. In no more than ten minutes he spotted movement on the hillside a couple hundred yards away. At his first glance, he suspected the lone figure to be wildlife, but he quickly saw that it was a human form. He immediately thought it was a Roman and moved aside, dropping into an oblong depression in the ground probably left by an age-old boulder, and viewed the man from out of sight.

But as he saw more details, he knew it was not a Roman at all. It was Adir.

Adir's strength had long since fled from his body. Baking under the hot sun, he trudged on through the hills, exhaustion and food and water deprivation leaving him in a haze. He repeated the monotonous thought to himself again and again just to put one foot in front of the other. His progress, however grueling, was steady and had endured unceasingly.

His sluggish senses were hesitant to react as a blurred form approached him. Finally, he realized what was happening and was instantly alarmed. He staggered back, but this only brought him to collapse where he stood. He groaned unintelligibly as it approached.

"It's me, Titus."

The phrase echoed in his mind until he understood and allowed his friend to come to his side.

Titus gripped Adir's left arm. He saw on his right arm a strip of cloth wrapped tightly around the sword wound he had received. It was sodded with blood and grime. Titus wrapped his other arm around Adir's back and took much of his companion's weight on his shoulders.

"We've got to get somewhere safe," Titus said to Adir as they staggered gradually upward. Titus grunted as he supported the weakening form of Adir. So much muscle was packed into Adir's lean body that Titus was soon breathing heavily with the task. The sun throbbed overhead as the two of them struggled up the slope.

Titus stopped, mopping sweat from his brow as he scanned the area ahead. He spotted a cave. They entered and Adir sighed and collapsed. Titus pulled the pack in front of him and pulled out the water skin that Adir had said was another gift of Eli. He tossed the skin to Adir, who had settled back in a corner of the cave.

"Drink all you need."

Adir nodded and smiled quickly. He gratefully unplugged the stopper and tipped up the skin. He swallowed a mouthful of water after swishing it in his mouth, and then another. He handed the skin back to Titus.

"Any food?"

Titus quickly produced a leftover piece of snake meat and handed it to Adir.

THE VICTOR PART II

"We'll stay in here until evening," Titus said. "You need the rest, and I doubt the Romans will come this way. I'm pretty sure I lost them a few miles back. Besides, if they find us, we run again. That's our lives now. Running."

"It's better than a life of fighting and killing."

There was silence till Titus changed the subject. "I think we better wash up your wound."

They busied themselves over Adir's arm for several minutes. The gash hurt terribly, but his other wounds were just as agonizing. The lingering wounds of the lions pained him, but perhaps worst of all was the wound he had thought had disappeared. When he sat forward, his muscles froze and his thoughts were drowned with pain. He wheezed and slightly convulsed as the small of his back overflowed with searing, devouring agony. The wound where Bacchus had nearly broken his spine in a tavern in Araby so long ago.

Titus looked on concernedly but knew he could not ease the pain. So, for the next few hours, they rested. Then, as evening came, Titus stirred.

"Where are you going?" asked Adir.

"To check for trouble around the cave. I'll be right back."

Titus left the cave and emerged into the dusk. He studied the surrounding area blanketed by the swarthy shades of the dropping sun. He moved up a couple of yards farther and checked around the cave. He was moving back when he heard a metallic *clink.* He cautiously crept in its direction, his heart beating a little faster.

Peeking over the crest of a hill, he was greeted by the sight of the Romans, spread down the slope, trotting after Valerius who led them. Titus crawled away and shuffled as fast as he dared back to the cave. He entered and crouched down, placing his hand on the hilt of his gladius where it poked out of the pack, and muttered to Adir.

"Romans."

His friend tensed in alarm. "Where?"

"Just over the next hill."

The studded boots of the legionnaires pounded the soil as the score of soldiers drew close.

Valerius was ordering his men about. They moved down the slope slowly, reluctantly. The soldiers were tired and discouraged. Titus was absolutely silent as they came within yards of the cave. He drew himself and the pack into the shadow. Adir was well concealed, having shifted behind a boulder poking out of the cave wall.

The moment was tense as the Romans passed. Yet they were startlingly unscrupulous in their search and the pair was left undiscovered. When the Romans were well past, Titus breathed a sigh of relief and relaxed.

"Well," Titus said, "with the Romans travelling away from us, I don't see any point of moving after them at the moment."

Adir smiled. "Nor do I," Adir agreed. "Let's sleep."

They woke early the next day. Titus was alert first and aroused Adir. It was dark, and though Adir was reluctant, he was on his feet in a few moments. He groaned as the pain resurfaced and he leaned against the cave wall, weakening.

Titus saw his friend's contorted face and knew the challenge that any physical activity would pose to Adir after yesterday. "We do not have to travel today. You need to recover."

Adir glowered at Titus. "No," he growled." He looked ragged, and his grimy skin and torn clothing added to his appearance of desolation. "We can't underestimate the Romans, especially not Quintus. For the sake of our journey, for the promise I made to God. I must do this."

Titus was quiet, then he chuckled. "Alright, then. Come."

Titus took the pack and they left the cave. The two moved through the hills, using precious little of their provisions, but making good time. They traced a path that wound up through the land. The minutes ticked away as they walked on, step by step, through the territory that Adir knew to be Asia Minor. Their progress was good, but they dared not slacken their pace at all. The miles rolled away beneath their feet.

Several hours after the sun pierced the horizon, just before noon, a town came into view. It was much the same as many of the other towns Adir visited, and the clump of a few dozen buildings was tucked into the bend of a river.

After a few moments, Adir said with finality, "Very well, in we go."

They walked up to the town.

Many of the women of the town had come to the well to collect water and discuss town affairs. They saw the two travelers approaching and a few surreptitiously slipped away to return quickly to their homes. A couple called to their husbands if their homes were near, and a few even offered timid greetings. Adir and Titus nodded to those and returned quick words of greeting and continued on their way to the community.

Adir and Titus were met by one of the women's husbands. He smiled warily to them at first, but then invited them into town.

"So, travelers," he commented.

"Yes," Adir replied.

"You, son, look like you have had a very bad couple of days."

"Exactly right."

THE VICTOR PART II

"And I can say a similar thing about you," he stated, glancing at Titus. "Well, you're welcome in our town."

Adir thanked him and they followed a dirt path into the marketplace at the center of town. He and Titus discussed their next move in low tones.

"What's the plan?" Titus asked.

"We tell them."

"What?"

"The truth. Our faith. Our stories. Christ."

"They'll kill us."

"They'll surely try."

Titus looked nervously at Adir. "And how do we bring up a conversation like that if it is illegal, and punishable by death?"

"We speak boldly and pray for the best. It worked when I met you."

The majority of the people now were coming in from their homes or from work to the market. A throng of people was growing around the stalls and booths that waited for their customers.

Adir shrugged at Titus. "Might as well do it."

He walked up to a booth. A large man smiled at him. He hesitated as he caught full sight of Adir, but in a moment regained his wits. "Can I help you, sir?"

Adir was suddenly speechless. "Uh…" He really didn't know where to start and could sense his embarrassment welling at his foolishness.

Finally, he scraped his thoughts together. Yet he still felt conspicuously inarticulate as he spoke again to the vendor behind the booth, who was growing impatient but had no other customers as an excuse to put an end to the fumbling conversation. "I would like to tell you of good news. Of Jes..."

Just then the vendor caught sight of the thin, spindly scars of puckered flesh that wrapped his shoulder, a souvenir of the lions that would have killed him if not for his God. The man spoke suddenly and halted Adir's speech as he saw them. "I do not mean to be rude, but if you don't mind me asking, what kind of folk are you and your friend?"

Adir took a deep breath and told them with as much confidence as he could muster, "We are Christians, sir." Titus took a sharp breath and came to Adir's side.

"What have you done?" he asked concernedly.

The man was spluttering at them, screaming for them to leave. "You will bring the wrath of Rome upon us! Be gone with your cult! We don't want your trouble in our town! Get out! Get out! Or you'll die like your leader did!"

As the crowd realized what was happening, they were swiftly becoming hostile towards Adir and Titus. One man yanked Adir forward roughly. Adir winced and the man snarled into his face, "Leave us, before you bring us all to our deaths."

"Yeah!" someone exclaimed in enthusiastic agreement.

Another man stepped forward, raising his hands to his fellow townsfolk. "I say we hear them out. We cannot become like Rome."

A stocky, angry looking citizen stepped out. "And I say you shut your blubbering lips, Antony, before I rip them off your face!"

Antony opened his mouth as if to reply, but received a fist to his jaw sending him retreating into the crowd. A mob was forming.

A woman's voice rang out, "Leave, snakes, and let us carry on!"

Adir raised his hands. "Very well." Adir knew they had to leave before the people turned violent.

Titus was close at his side as they trotted out of the town, darting out the quickest exit of the village.

"They hate us," Titus said, gloomily bringing the obvious to light.

"Rome has made its subjects scared, and wounded. Their countries have been humbled, their lives bent to the will of Caesar. Our faith costs lives, and not just our own. They know that, and I do not blame them, though I pity them."

Adir and Titus travelled on, occasionally mentioning the incident or another from their journey, but most often finding solace in silence. Adir knew that the Mediterranean coast was only a dozen or so miles to their west, and as they were travelling south now, he knew as well that there would undoubtedly be more towns to appear. He mentioned this to Titus.

"Will we enter those too?"

"Yes."

"And if they try to kill us?"

"We try not to die."

So they walked on. Eventually, gradually, and without any effort otherwise, their pace began to slow. Before long it was late afternoon. And still there were no signs of anything other than the wilderness. They travelled yet further. And still, nothing. The thick veil of night was unravelling across the land. Time crawled away. Then, they were in darkness. "Adir," Titus said firmly, "we must stop."

Adir waited. "Please," Titus said. "We can't keep this up for long, not in pitch black, especially considering your wounds."

"I say we keep going. Titus, have faith. We go on, or at least I do. With or without you, I continue."

Titus sighed. "Very well."

Adir walked on, and as he rose over a hill, saw in the distance a speck of light. But it was gone too quick, and he did not even know if he had really seen it. Yet he plunged on with more enthusiasm. Titus was close behind him, scanning the blackness for anything. Adir climbed another hill and looked out again. His heart leapt.

"Titus, a village."

They advanced on the clump of houses. As they reached the outskirts of the community, they were noticed by a man who sat on the porch of his small house. His hands were working busily, laboring at a block of wood in one hand with a knife in the other.

"Who are you?" he asked them.

"Travelers," Titus said. "We are weary and footsore and in need of rest. But we are poor as well. I'm afraid we can offer no pay."

The man sat brooding for a moment. "There's an old widow that lives up that way." He pointed. "I'm sure she'll accommodate you. She's never turned anyone down. Her house has a garden in front. You can't miss it."

Titus and Adir said their thanks and headed for the house. Just as the man had said, they spotted the garden almost immediately. Adir walked up to the door and knocked. They waited a while before it was answered. The door opened slowly and the old lady's kind, warm face peeked out at them. She looked them over and sighed. "Looks like you've had a bad time."

Adir smiled. "We've been travelling this way, and a man told us you may grant us a rest in your house. We understand if you cannot do so, but.."

"Oh, no! Come on in!"

ANDREW MEADE

They were ushered into the home. They conversed meekly for a little while. The widow, who said her name was Miriam, hurried around her house. She brought them some bread and figs, and just as quickly served watered down, cheap, but rather tasteful, wine in rough wooden cups. All the while, they offered her warm thanks for the kindness. She simply smiled and continued.

Miriam, after a few minutes, said she would do something about their clothing. She departed and upon her return offered Adir and Titus both a rough brown tunic. "Those were my husband's. I'll take your other clothes and wash them, and see if I cannot attend to some of the rips and such."

They changed and handed over their old clothes to Miriam. With a stifled exclamation she saw his wounds and scars.

"Young man, I'm afraid I must insist that I help your injuries.

So for many more minutes she dressed his wounds. She muttered on a few occasions that there had been a broken arm and rib, and trauma to his spine that had never been properly healed. He did not explain to her the circumstances under which he sustained the injuries. He did however say that there had been a man in the desert and a man who ran a tavern that had done a good job of treating him.

"They may have saved your life, and thanks to them for that, but you never fully healed, and I suspect the back is still giving you problems now, eh?"

"Quite right."

She finally finished with him, and, after checking over Titus, led them to where she had laid out pallets for them to sleep. Adir and Titus slept through the night with no disturbances, and they awoke the next day well rested and surprisingly eager to begin speaking of their faith. Adir was genuinely enthralled with the strangely wonderful prospect, and even Titus was surprised to find himself excited for the task at hand.

The two were still beginning to stir from their pallets when Miriam shuffled in.

"A meal is waiting for you in the front room. It's not much, but it's food."

They went to the front room and, happy with the food before them, ate swiftly. When they finished, Adir told Miriam they would go around the town for a while.

Once they left the small house, again thanking Miriam, they instinctively headed for the center of town.

It was not a lively village, but they soon found that even this obscure village had some fantastic goods to be sold. But of course, they had no money. As they walked around the market, Adir saw stables. He turned to Titus and asked, "Would you not agree we need those horses?"

""Yes," Titus said before snapping back, "But have you forgotten that we have no money, and people despise Christians?""

"Perhaps one thing to outweigh this is the hatred of Rome's rule, and the love of their gladiators."

Titus puffed his cheeks and his eyes widened.

"I won respect and fame for my fighting," Adir said. "I might as well use it for something good."

It had worked once for Adir, but he did not know if it would work again. He entered the small building just adjacent the stables and approached the only man inside.

"Can I interest you in business?" he asked. "I have some fine horses and great prices."

"I'm not quite looking for any great horse, but I would like to see your cheapest, that can still run hard and far."

"All my beasts will do that. But the cheapest, you say?" He scratched his stubbly chin. "Follow me."

He directed Adir out of the building and pointed to a horse in a far stall. It was squat, and comparatively poorly groomed. "Thirty sestertii, and I assure you, it's a good horse, and a good deal."

"I don't have any sestertii."

THE VICTOR PART II

"Well, as this is a Roman province, you would normally be expected to pay in that currency, but I could accept another."

"I… I have no money."

The man glared at him coldly. "Do you take me for a fool? What kind of ignorant moron would come in here, ask for one of my horses, and then when I offer him to you, tell me that you have no money?"

"I just… I need the horse."

"Then pay for it."

"I can't, but I…"

"Well, I am surprised. A gladiator as famous as yourself should be able to get a horse."

Adir was dumbfounded and slightly alarmed that he was so recognizable. "I didn't think you would notice so quickly."

"I recognized you the moment you walked through my door. And you arrogant, greedy Roman pig! You think you can have one of my horses just because you fought in the arena? I know that was what you were planning, wasn't it. Just like you Romans. I went to one of your fights, and all I saw was a boy drenched in innocent blood and soaking up the glory that came with it."

Adir was silent. "Yes," he finally managed to say. "But I beg of you, I need the horse, and I'm not who you think I am."

"Why do you need it so much?"

197

"Because I'm running. I escaped and now I'm a Christian and I'm being hunted by the Romans. I hate them just as much as you do, and now I need that horse."

"A Christian, eh? Well, first of all, don't give me any of that religious waste, or I will kill you."

The cold sincerity frightened Adir.

"And it is true that I hate Rome. I may be able to help you."

Adir smiled lightheartedly. "Can you help my poverty-stricken fugitive friend as well?"

"WHAT?" he roared in comic exasperation.

Adir and the stable owner haggled for several more minutes before they finally reached an agreement.

"Alright," the owner said, "I can give you both a donkey, but don't expect anything spectacular from them. First though, I need you to fetch me water from the well, muck out the stalls, and water my horses."

"Gladly," Adir said, bobbing his head, and knowing full well the favor the stable owner was doing.

"Oh, and bring your friend. I have a wild horse out in the corral. I want to see him ride it. I might as well get some entertainment from all of this."

Adir brought Titus to the stable owner and they left for the corral. Then, without many events of consequence, Adir set out upon his ordained chores, most of a full day's work.

Only a few minutes after Adir had watered the last horse, and as he sat resting, Titus and the stable owner returned, apparently having done a good enough job of taming the wild horse for a day. Adir offered some water left in the bucket he had used to Titus so he could clean off some of the mud on him from the experience.

"So you finished your work?" the man asked Adir.

"Yes."

The stable owner gave them their donkeys and sent them on their way.

They walked the donkeys back to Miriam's house. They loosely tied up the donkeys at the back of the house, on a fence, and went back to the door. Miriam smiled at them when she opened it.

"Your clothes are ready. Cleaned and repaired as best as I could manage, but you can keep the clothes I gave you."

"Thank you," Adir said and they went inside.

They changed into their old clothes, packing the others as spares. They were just about to leave when Miriam implored them to let her cook one more meal for them. They ate well, and then set off. They threw blankets on their donkeys' backs and tried to compensate for a proper saddle the best they could. Then, they mounted and rode silently away from the lonely town.

THE VICTOR PART II

CHAPTER FIFTEEN

They travelled on, down the easterly coast of the Mediterranean, urging their mounts on further and further, and eating away the miles at a steady pace each day. They knew the Romans were close at hand and this kept them from slowing at all. Titus had only a faint idea of what they were heading for, but at the moment he was content to know nothing more than the task of travelling south.

It was a grueling ordeal, but they were happy to find the donkeys were of good breed and the plucky little beasts plodded on, day after day, week after week, through the worst terrain and the most pleasant. The two men scrounged for what food they could obtain, while the donkeys ate the grass that had not begun to die in the face of the coming winter.

Their travels soon fell into a rigid routine, interrupted only by drastic changes in the terrain or by coming upon a town or village. There Adir and Titus would deliver their message, and say what they had to say of faith and the Good News in Christ. Some would listen, while others would scoff or react violently. They never fully converted anyone in these towns, but they did what they could, and planted the seed. It was up to Christ what would become of it.

One day Adir and Titus lay on the banks of a stream where they had filled their water skins and took an icy dip in the frigid water. They were bare-chested while their tunics dried beside them. The cool air on their wet skin was refreshing after the hard travelling. Titus then spoke, for his curiosity had spiked.

"Why are we heading south? What are we looking for down there?"

"Malachi. I won't, I can't, believe that he's dead and I'm going to find him."

Titus nodded. He understood and he was going to help.

They conversed only a little about the topic before moving on to others and it was mentioned sparingly any more while they travelled.

He knew what city to go to, and he figured finding Malachi could be easy.

Almost a month after they left the town where they had received the donkeys they entered into Araby. After receiving a long overdue map from a farmer, they found the city without mishap.

They asked around about Malachi, and nearly everyone remembered the lightning strike in the tavern and the intervention by the Romans. He was directed to an obviously unfrequented path that wound away from the city into the distance where they were told Malachi had been living for the past few months. He had been wounded when he faced the Romans and had to rent out the tavern, as he was unable to attend to it any longer. Physicians still tended to him on a regular basis and he was beginning to recover.

They went up the path and tethered their donkeys outside of Malachi's present house. Adir knocked and was answered by Malachi's maid.

"Malachi does not accept many visitors."

"Just tell him Adir is here to see him."

She disappeared and returned to say, "Malachi welcomes you."

"I'll wait outside." Adir was about to protest, but he was cut off. "Do what you must, but I am no part of this, and I will not intrude. This is for you, not I."

Adir nodded and followed the maid. She led him through the house to Malachi's room. And there, in the bed, Adir could see by the dim light a face aged twenty years by the grim wound opened in his chest. Bandages were clumped around it, stained with blood. His face was white and his form seemed frail and stricken by what had befallen him. Adir's once strong, vibrant friend was weak and struggling before him. Malachi smiled falteringly, his thin, tight lips curling up only slightly. His voice was shaky and rough, but there was an undoubted note of the old Malachi, the great man Adir had known a few months before. Adir smiled as the familiar voice spoke to him.

"Ah, Adir, it is wonderful to see you. I thought you were dead. Then again, I had thought I was dead at the moment. I suppose I am happily mistaken on both accounts."

His body was wracked with violent coughing and his thin frame shuddered. He winced at the pain and it took him a few moments to compose himself before he could speak again.

"I must apologize for the shape I'm in," he said. "Only a few days ago I went into an operation on my wound. Bako is a wonderful physician, but it did more to my health than had been accounted for. But I am alive, and I am recovering. That alone is enough to keep me happy. The wound was bad, fatal. I should have died. In fact, there's no explanation to how I lived. The bloody Roman sword went through a good part of my ribcage and went deep, almost hit my heart, Bako says. The only thing I really know is that some Roman slashed me and left as if I was dead. A shame, too. I could have won. He was the last one left. I was in a bad way for a long time. I had lost a lot of blood and what I had left in me was barely moving. Breathing was blasted near impossible and the whole world was just a haze for so long. Almost a month, I think. I drifted interminably between being unconscious or coming into a world where I was lost and immobilized. I drank hardly enough to survive and ate hardly anything. Then, I was beginning to be conscious for longer and was making a recovery. The physicians kept tending me, and still do, and I'm healing."

"It's great that you're healing, but the wound, all of it, I never meant…"

"Oh, shut it!" Adir was taken aback, but Malachi just chuckled slightly. "I don't blame any of it on you. I blame those vile Roman dogs. You, boy are really something, and I will never regret that I threw four Roman fools into the dust, even if the fifth did split open my chest cavity like a walnut. Or, I guess a chestnut."

Adir laughed at the absurdity and good humor with which Malachi was handling it all. He thanked Malachi. "But what happened to all the Romans who came here to catch me?" he asked.

"They got what was due them. Araby isn't even their land anyway, and some bandits didn't like the idea of having legionnaires coming in on their territory. They rode in and sent the Romans scampering off with their tails between their legs. I must say, that was the first time I've seen most of a community come out of their homes to cheer a gang of desert bandits returning from a raid.

"So," Malachi asked, "how did you come to stand before me? Last I heard the Romans had chased you off the edge of a cliff and captured you in one of their ships."

Adir began to relate the tale of his journey from his capture on the ship to his return to Malachi. Malachi listened thoughtfully and smiled to Adir when he was done.

"You really are fantastic, aren't you?" he said laughingly.

"Christ is."

Malachi's lips turned up at the edges in a kind of smile but he did nothing else until he finally spoke.

"I never really believed, you know. In the months you spent with me I never had any part of your faith, but I think it changed me, Adir. And after all the days in a haze I'm a very different man. So why not start fresh? Why not believe? Christ has been right in front of my face this whole time but I never looked at Him. I want to now. I want to believe. You lived in my tavern, and you were so steadfast and faithful. Even then you weren't really a believer, but you knew Christ was doing something. I want to know Christ, Adir."

The conversation continued for at least another hour, the two speaking of matters of faith and of more trivial issues. It again seemed to Adir like he was back in the months where he lived in the tavern. But he was not, and the visit finally drew to an end. Adir withdrew from Malachi's room after a

THE VICTOR PART II

long, sincere farewell. Adir and Titus agreed not to stay any longer, and were prepared to set off again when the maid called Adir once again into Malachi's room.

"I want to help your journey. I've talked to my attendants, and we'll give you some supplies. Also, how would you like some proper horses instead of those old donkeys? I'll take them for two of my horses. And I think you'll remember Zo, eh? Well, I got her back, and I offer her to you again."

And so, amid numerous thanks, Adir and Titus' supplies were well replenished and they received the horses. As Adir mounted Zo, and Titus a fine brown horse, they faced the predicament of where to go next. Adir voiced this issue and Titus responded.

"Where you go, I'll gladly come along. I am with you on this journey, but it is still your journey."

"Very well. I'm heading back to Egypt."

Adir reined in Zo by the hut before him about a week later. A long strip of cloth was wound about his head to protect him from the swirling dust and sand that had raged about them in the desert windstorm. He had similarly outfitted Zo's head. Titus and his horse were identically shrouded in the turban-like fashion. The sandstorm had been ferocious. It lashed the bodies of they and their horses hour after hour, as it had off and on for almost two days.

Adir was overjoyed and relieved they had not lost their way as he spotted Matthias' hut. As he directed Zo to approach, he noticed immediately that an awning had recently been constructed onto the back of the hut, and sheltering under it was a horse. Adir for the moment disregarded it and tethered Zo under the awning as Titus did the same thing. After situating the horses, Adir approached the door of the hut, and there he encountered a puzzling thing. The once dilapidated hut was noticeably well kept, as was the meager landscaping, though it was being eradicated by the storm. Someone was quite certainly living here.

So Adir knocked. And the door was answered. The new tenant of the hut pushed the door only slightly ajar so as to not blow in much sand. He looked over the two travelers, opening the door wider and ushering them hastily in. Adir and Titus entered and unwrapped their heads. They were disheveled and covered in dust. "Shake it off and I'll sweep it out," the occupant told them. They did so and were then left in an awkward silence.

"Take a seat."

Adir perched on a stool and Titus on another. Then, Adir began to notice a familiarity in the man's voice. He had once known him well, that he was certain of. He looked up into the man's face.

THE VICTOR PART II

His features were crowded by a massive, unkempt beard and shoulder-length shaggy hair, but he was recognizable. Adir was dumbfounded. "Diomed."

"Indeed."

Yes, it was him. But he was no longer the fat, stern gladiator trainer. His body was hardened, and he was strangely happy.

"Adir. I thought you would come, but I was never really sure. Well, I'm a Christian now. I ran away from the ludus after Semerkhet... well, you heard, right?"

"Yes."

"Well, after he died, an angel came to me. Really indescribable, but it changed me. I came here. I've been growing in Christ and taking over what old Matthias had been doing for decades. The luxuries of my old life have abandoned me and made me a better man, a better believer, for it. And, well, I'm ready for an adventure, if you're okay with me tagging along."

"Of course.'

"However, we can't do anything with this storm still going," Titus said.

"He's right. We'll have to wait it out."

"And, Adir, I need to tell you, Matthias left something for you."

Diomed scoured the small hut for a moment before he found what he was looking for, a small leather pouch. He showed Adir the number of scrolls within it.

"These are lengths of Scripture. Scrolls from the old Jewish compilations of their records. And letters Christians wrote to one another. The letters detail the life of Jesus, the works of His apostles, and their wisdom to believers. I've been reading them, but he left them for you."

"I thank you." Adir took the pouch and added to it the scroll of David's psalms before setting it aside for the moment.

"And who is this?" Diomed finally asked, gesturing to Titus.

"This is Primus Imperious Titus. And, Titus, I believe I've told you of Diomed."

"Yes."

"Well, Primus, how did you come to travel with Adir?"

"I go by Titus. Primus Imperious is my family name."

"I like Primus better."

"Okay. And I came to travel with Adir because I, too, am a Christian. I was a legionnaire when I came across the faith. I certainly didn't believe it at first, and didn't for a long time, but as I came to accept it, I knew there was nothing but truth to be found in the faith. I was captured by pirates but escaped and encountered Adir in Graecia. I've been travelling with him since then."

THE VICTOR PART II

The three talked for a while, and then went out to check on the horses. By then, it was nearly time to sleep, for they had arrived late. Adir and Titus settled down on their bedrolls adjacent Diomed's pallet, and after a quick meal which hardly could be considered a real dinner, they fell swiftly asleep.

When they awoke, the storm had thankfully passed. They ate again and checked once more on the horses. After this, Titus and Diomed entered the hut. Adir lingered outside.

"So, where do we go?" Diomed asked.

"Up to Adir, I guess."

"Sounds fine by me."

Titus frowned and hung his head. "I'm not even sure if I will go."

"What?"

"I mean, we've spoken enough of Christ. I think we deserve more of a rest than we've had."

"Diomed scowled. "You—why , how?"

" Just think… we've done enough."

Diomed was glowering at Titus, his contempt growing on his face. "How can you turn so quickly from the faith? How could you desert it?"

"You know not what it is like to face adversity in your faith. All you've done is cower in this old hut and read letters."

They were silenced as Adir entered, indignant. "Stop fighting, you fools. We're all new believers. We have no idea what we are doing, not one of us

211

does. Don't turn us into hypocrites. And Diomed, please shave your face. You look like a beast."

Adir stepped outside again, and this time Titus followed him.

"I apologize."

"Don't. Not to me. We all have endured much, and in too many ways I am thinking the same thing you are, but I know it is not true, and I will not change my path."

Adir walked around the hut to a grave. It was Matthias'. Titus left him alone to pray over the grave.

A few minutes later, he entered the hut with the other two, Diomed clean shaven and somber.

"Adir, I have something else for you," he said.

He went to his pack in the corner of the room and removed a sword, in its scabbard. Adir recognized it immediately. Diomed pulled the blade out a few inches and then replaced it, handing the weapon to Adir.

"Why do you have this?"

"For you."

"I don't need to carry a sword. I have faith."

"We can't do anything for God if we're dead."

"If it is the will of God, He will prevent that."

"That doesn't mean we should place ourselves in the way of death. I think it is our responsibility to prevent our death as well."

Adir was about to protest, but Diomed cut him off. "Just take the sword."

Adir thought, and decided against further prolonging the row.

Then, he spoke calmly and surely.

"Both of you know what you are doing if you choose to come. There will be a reward in your faith, but it cannot be guaranteed in this life. What will be guaranteed is hardship, and trials. As soon as we leave this place, there may not be another moment of peace in our lives for years to come. Do you understand this? The people, they will try to hunt us, kill us. They will hate us, and they will strive to destroy us. But God loves us all, He made us all, and Christ died for us all. We have to always continue. There will be misery, hardship as you cannot imagine, but Christ will be with us through it all. Consider it a warning and a promise."

CHAPTER SIXTEEN

It was midmorning when the three led their mounts through the delta of the Nile, and as they cantered out onto one of the roads that led to Alexandria, they could see the city in the distance. They had decided when they left that this would be their destination. Only a few days ago they had arrived at Matthias' old hut and now their horses trotted through the gates of Alexandria.

They had also preordained their route once they reached the city. They were to head to the center and, upon arrival, speak from there. Diomed had suggested that they speak at the revered Museum and Library of Alexandria, but they had soon decided against it. Schools, libraries and religious establishments they decided would be best avoided at first. Diomed had visited Alexandria often and led the way through the city as they wound their way among the narrow streets and alleys, away from the main avenues of the city. Soon, they were in the central square.

But, as always, they had no idea where to begin. They tethered their horses in a backstreet and discussed it away from the crowd and busy atmosphere of the square.

Suddenly, Diomed chuckled and smiled wryly.

"We're in Egypt."

"Yes," Adir said unsurely.

"Semerkhet was always very popular."

"Yes." Adir could already see what he was thinking, and was growing more and more apprehensive.

"As were his gladiators—as were you."

"Yes—well…" Adir began to protest, but Diomed laughed it by.

"How hard can it be?"

Diomed hastened out into the crowd. He grabbed a random crate where it leaned up against a building and placed it amid the crowd. He stepped up on it and looked out over the people. He was already a head taller than most, and now he towered over everyone.

"Do you know who I am?" His voice boomed and rang out over the crowd. They quieted and began to focus on him. Murmurs rippled through the crowd. They were puzzled.

"I am Diomed, the trainer of gladiators for Semerkhet. You remember Semerkhet, don't you?"

The crowd was filled with shouts of affirmation.

"Do you remember his fighters? Do you remember Adir? Do you remember the Killer of the East?"

The crowd was erupting into cries of interspersed disdain and admiration.

ANDREW MEADE

"Here he is!"

Diomed jumped down and hastily herded Adir onto the crate. Stunned and conflicted, Adir sluggishly stepped up. And his mind cleared. He knew what he had to do. He hadn't the least idea how he was going to do it, but it was nonetheless the task before him.

"You're a Christian, aren't you?" someone roared.

"Yes I am." He could almost feel in the air that those words were a death sentence, as they basically were.

"You're a rotten Christian fool, that's what you are!" came another shout, this one violently slurred. A man burst from the knot of people around Adir and lunged, but was stopped abruptly. Diomed had stepped up and threw his arm out in front of the man's chest, hating his approach suddenly.

"Back," Diomed said coldly.

Wheezing from the shock of the impact, the man staggered away.

"Why are you a Christian?"

Adir struggled to find a statement that would tell the whole truth and sway the beliefs of these people. But as he puzzled over his next words, he fell upon a simple conclusion. If people were to believe the Good News, it would not be by the presentation or the tact of those who told them. If he was to convince them it could only be through the truth and power in the gospel of Christ.

"Because it is the truth and the grace of God has proven himself time and time again."

"But how?"

"Miracles. Jesus Christ was killed but *rose from the dead.* Miracles are everywhere. I've certainly experienced enough of them. Miracles are always there, and so is Christ."

He spoke for a few minutes longer, telling of miracles and the power of Christ, and most of the crowd dispersed. Finally, he stepped down and he and his two companions retreated to the alley where their horses were. They untied them and led them a little farther away from the square.

"Where are we going?" Titus asked.

"A home," Diomed replied, "of a Christian. They sometimes meet there, the believers. It seems a fitting place to go. I only just remembered it. It's been so long since I stayed in Alexandria for any length of time."

Twenty minutes later, the three had put their horses a block or so away, tethering them to a dilapidated windowsill in the rundown part of the city. Adir knocked on the door of the Christian's home. A middle-aged man opened the door for them to enter. They introduced themselves and he told them his name was Adom. They told him of

ANDREW MEADE

their journey and why they were in Alexandria, and he was happy to have them.

"And you've come on a good day. In an hour or so some other believers will be coming. It seems you've already made an impression in the square. So settle in for the time being." They did so, and in an hour, just as Adom had said, other Christians arrived. Gathered together, the dozen or so believers worshipped. And it was wonderful. Adir could feel the Spirit moving among them and felt the joy of praise in Him.

It was simple, but wonderful. It was as the Apostles had said in their letters. Where believers gathered together, there was power.

Adir did not know how long it was. An hour or two, but when they finished, it was after noon. The Christians were starting to leave when a quick knock hit the door. Before it was even answered the door was pushed open and a woman stumbled in. In her arms was a small boy, his body limp. Tears streamed down the woman's face.

"He... he was sick..." she sobbed. "I think he died!" Her hysterical voice cracked and she fell to her knees, staring vacantly at the boy's face. "You're followers of Christ," she said weakly. "He could heal people, bring them back. You can, too!" She looked desperately around at the faces in the room. "Please."

THE VICTOR PART II

Everyone seemed too stunned to do anything. And so Adir stepped forward.

"Yes," he said. "The power of Christ can do amazing things. I will help you."

Adir's thoughts were in turmoil for a brief moment but he calmed himself. He remembered what he read in one of Matthias' scrolls. That with faith, anything is possible. Anything can be done in the power of Christ if you utterly believe.

He cleared his mind, thinking only of the miracles and power of Jesus, and he placed his hand on the boy's chest. "Christ heals you," he whispered, and took his hand away.

A long, tense moment ensued, but in time the boy drew a shaky breath and opened his eyes. The woman gasped and smiled at the boy. She thanked Adir and left, praising God.

For a moment there was silence. There was no mention of what had just transpired, but those who were about to leave settled in again and the worship resumed because of the miracle. They all knew the gravity of it, and were happy to share in the awe in silence and singing praises.

The news must have travelled fast, for in another hour a crowd gathered around the house. They were curious people, wanting to know more about the miracle and Adir. Adir spoke to them, but he was grateful that the other Christians could as well. Many were turned away by the strange message that was offered to them, but some lingered. And Adir felt good. He was serving Christ. Nobody converted, but they were hearing the Gospel, and that was as much as they could do.

Amid all this, Titus slipped away. He was feeling restless after being cooped up in the house for hours. He trotted down the cobblestone street, happy to be in the relatively fresh air, away from the monotony of the worship. In a few minutes he found himself maybe a block away from the house, in the slums. A year ago he would have felt disconcerted here, but he found now that he was accustomed to it. He passed a beggar, remembering his time spent in that Grecian port town. He looked thoughtfully at the figure hunched against the wall. He had nothing to offer him. In all practical purposes, he was in poverty himself. And yet he felt compelled to speak to him. As he approached though, the matter was ripped from his control entirely.

The beggar erected himself in a flash, and before Titus could think, he was already lunging for him. Titus felt shaking arms grasp him, and bodily force him into the side of the building. The beggar crammed his face close to Titus' and spoke in harsh tones, foul breath coiling in Titus' nostrils and hissing through rotten, chipped teeth. "You're a Christian, aren't ye?"

THE VICTOR PART II

Titus spoke truthfully, deciding that no immediate harm could come from the man.

"I am."

The beggar stepped back, and yanking up the long sleeve on his ratty tunic revealed a gruesome patch of leprosy.

"I ain't even s'posed to be in the city. You can heal me, eh?"

Titus was taken aback. He was unsure, but strove to keep it from showing on his face. "Yes," he said, mustering the last resolve he had.

"Do it."

Titus haltingly placed a hand on the beggar's shoulder, and closed his eyes. He lifted his heart to his Lord, and desperately sought the power to heal this man. He was fumbling, and deep inside of him his uncertainty was growing. But he forced it aside, and leaning on the God that had always saved him, he began to pray. But always, lurking somewhere in his heart, was the single thought, that maybe he couldn't do it, maybe God couldn't do it.

"Jesus, heal him."

Titus glanced at the beggar, his mind filling with trepidation. The patch of the terrible disease remained. Again Titus prayed, but the doubt remained, this time more infectious, and it wouldn't leave him.

"Lord, heal this man!"

But nothing happened.

"Liar!"

Titus looked into the man's eyes. There were tears there. He had been desperate. Now he was hopeless. He turned and left, sobbing. As he passed out of sight his wails could be heard, and Titus was racked with shock.

Adir heard shouting suddenly. He looked into the clump of people around the home. A man had approached them, screaming curses. "Are you Christians now?" he exclaimed. "Are you with that cult? Get out of our city!"

A dozen more men were appearing from alleys and side-streets, forming around the people before the home. The mob's intentions were evident. Some held planks of wood, chains, whatever they could find, while most were prepared to fight with their fists. Adir did not see the first attack, but in an instant the gang had rushed the others, striking out ferociously. Among the group who had come to hear the Christians, the more hostile gathered weapons wherever they could, or lashed out with balled fists to defend themselves. Cries and moans of those who were injured echoed in the narrow street, while the thump of a fist striking hard against flesh drummed in the air. The harassed people were fighting back hard now, and soon the riot swarmed throughout the street. More people were emerging into the tumult of thrashing bodies and wheeling

THE VICTOR PART II

limbs. Adir was stunned at the scene before him. What could he do? The smell of blood tainted the air, and his senses prickled as he heard cries of pain. The mad, furious crush of people, dozens locked in mortal combat, was all around him. Suddenly, he was being swept into the fray. Limbs flew around him, pummeling him, but he managed to ignore them.

"This has to stop!" He shouted, almost to himself.

But he could do nothing to prevail against the mob. It was almost evening and the sun, as it was beginning to set, sent garish shades of crimson spilling over the violence heightening the infernal ordeal. Adir saw one man pounce on another, striking again and again. Then, blood dripping from his knuckles, he smiled maliciously at his victim and cocked back his fist to deliver the death blow. Adir lunged forward and barreled into the aggressor, heaving him back and sending him sprawling on the flagstone.

Adir turned, scanning the scene, when a fist hurtled into his head. His skull filled with flashes of light, and he felt himself thrown back. His head throbbed and blood poured from his nose, but he kept his wits about him and dodged the next blow. He retaliated sharply, striking into the midriff, but this was only meant to stun his opponent, long enough to subdue him. He shoved him back, and the man staggered away. Adir began to push his way through the crowd, back to the house. The chaos churning around him was tragic. He saw projectiles whirling through the air into the crowd and surrounding buildings, some on fire.

Adir emerged again and scanned the edges of the riot for Diomed. The big man was some yards away, helping a few others drag a toppled wagon into place as a barricade. Adir hurried over to him. With the wagon situated, he turned and Adir spoke urgently.

"Where's Titus?"

"He left."

Adir muttered in frustration. His mind was in shambles, and he could do nothing but witness the violence.

Titus could hear the riot, and he was for a moment conflicted, then, as thoughts came to him, he quickly discerned his course of action. He would get to his horse and flee Alexandria. He cleared his mind of all else but self-preservation. He would run.

He sprinted down the avenue and skirted the block onto one of the main streets. He remembered that this main artery of the city branched into another street nearby, and in one of the dank alleys along that stretch of buildings they had put their horses.

THE VICTOR PART II

He ran down and made the turn, but stopped suddenly. The edges of the riot had bled through into this neighborhood. The horses' alley was in sight. But before he could act he heard it. The one noise that paralyzed him with fear and scrambled his mind where he stood. A hundred studded sandals marching in unison. He looked down the street to see a unit of Praetorians dressed for war, and at their head, Quintus.

Adir froze when he heard the sound of the Romans. His heart sank. He looked at Diomed.

"We have to get as many people out of here as we can. A lot of them are going to die. We have to save the ones we can."

Diomed left Adir's side to evacuate anybody who would listen. "Flee! Flee! The Romans are here! Soldiers are coming!"

Adir ran away from the riot and into the Christian home. Finding his pack, he unsheathed his falcata, the lethal curved sword of Greek design, and exited. He stuck close to the buildings, evading most of the fighting. He came out on the main street, the riot raging behind him. And ahead, the Romans slowly advanced.

He saw Titus ahead of him, ducking into a side-street away from the soldiers and between the buildings caught flashes of him sprinting away. A mounted soldier approached Quintus. He bent low

225

in his saddle to speak to his superior. Apparently Quintus gave him orders, for the soldier, who Adir quickly recognized as Valerius, nodded and lead his horse away, disappearing behind the column of Praetorians.

Quintus grinned maniacally at the scene of the riot. In his booming voice he shouted to his soldiers. But his voice was tainted with blind rage and abandon. His words were careless and brutal. Then, he began his orders. "The first century, you advance with me straight into the riot. The other units, box it in. Move in slowly, but lose no ground. The horsemen have circled the area, the whole place is ringed in, three blocks all around. No one escapes. THEY WILL LEARN OF ROME'S WRATH! THEY ALL DIE TODAY!"

Titus sprinted through the backstreets of Alexandria. He slowly wheeled back when he heard the clatter of hooves in the next street. He ran for all he could and clambered through the door of the Christian house. He snatched up his gladius and just as quickly fled again. He could see a Roman standing just outside the door. He again ran back through the streets, this time weaving his way between the buildings, seeking another passage away from the epicenter of the chaos. And again he heard hooves striking hard against the flagstone. He ducked into an alley and moved away as quietly as he could. But it was no use. Three others were fleeing down the same street, and the horseman ran them down in seconds as they entered the alley. Titus scrambled away as Valerius slashed down at the people from the back of his horse. Gore splattered the walls of the alley.

Valerius snarled and brandished his blood-soaked gladius. He struck his horse's flanks with his heels and charged Titus. The latter marveled at a conveniently placed crate and took hold of it. He heaved it onto his forearm and lifted it as a shield. Valerius slowed his horse and chuckled at the attempt. He jabbed his gladius into the planking, and wrenching it away, ripped off the crate. And yet, the top still remained firmly in Titus' grasp, as good a shield as ever. Valerius again spurred on his horse and Titus shrank against the wall to avoid the lethal juggernaut. As he passed, Valerius stabbed into Titus' shield again. The motion of ripping away the crate was repeated and the makeshift shield was flung away into the air.

The force threw Titus down onto the flagstone, desperately hacking at Valerius as he passed. Yet the narrow alley made maneuvering the horse nearly impossible and this gave Titus the crucial time he needed to regain his footing and run. He was panicked, and barely computed that his mad dash was sending him back towards the riot.

Quintus lingered in his place after the soldiers had moved out around the riot, which fell into a panic rather than the rage that had so far dominated most of its violence.

"Leave the Arab kid. He's mine."

The soldiers moved around Adir, and he remained motionless. The two stood, staring each other down, locked in fixity. Quintus took a step forward. Adir mimicked him. The process repeated. Then, Adir spoke.

"You're a monster, you know."

"No, I'm a necessary evil."

Adir heard an eruption of agony ripple through the crowd behind him. He cocked his head down, listening grimly. He did not look, but he was certain that the Roman shield wall had met the crowd and was moving in on all sides. The short, lethal blades of the gladius would dart out from behind a shield and cut deep in a flash of cold metal and hot blood. His breath was ragged and his blood burned at the thought of the slaughter behind him. But again, the grim realization. He could do nothing.

Quintus was walking in full stride, circling Adir slowly. Adir did not move but kept a cold glare nailed to Quintus. He wanted nothing more than to fight Quintus now, and he knew Quintus wanted the same. He mused at the thought.

"Stop your soldiers," he hissed sharply.

"What?"

THE VICTOR PART II

"Stop your soldiers and I'll fight you. My life if you just stop the soldiers. Tell your men to hold their lines. Stop the advance. And you can fight me, execute me, tear me apart. Just do it."

Quintus smirked. "If you hadn't turned into a stupid Christian, I might have liked you. But now, I would like to kill you."

"It's a mutual sentiment."

"Yes. So I'll call off the Praetorians." He paused. "Halt the advance! Hold your lines!"

"I thank you."

Quintus laid aside his plumed helmet and gilded buckler.

"Even," he growled.

He resumed pacing around Adir, who now turned to face him. He felt a knot of fury in his chest, sending power crackling down his limbs to the tips of his fingers. Righteous anger swelled inside of him and he knew he could beat Quintus.

"So," the latter said, "The greatest gladiator and the greatest soldier in all of the Empire. This shall be interesting."

"Indeed."

Titus emerged onto the street and wheeled around quickly. But it was too late. Valerius was close behind him, on foot.

"Stop," Titus said. "I'm not a Christian. I'm not part of this. Just let me go."

229

"You think I've forgotten you? I remember you. You're a traitor and a fugitive."

"But, please, you have to believe me." Titus threw up his hands and dropped his sword. "Please."

Valerius laughed and lunged, ramming the boss of his shield into Titus' face, and the young man's world went black.

The fight began explosively. Quintus leaped across the distance to Adir and slashed down. Adir parried and stepped back, jerking his body away from Quintus' second attack. He saw Quintus' blade shooting out at him and flicked his own blade around to block. The two swords chopped and stabbed through the air, but each blow was unsuccessful. Sparks flew as the blades clashed and the lengths of metal shrieked and rasped against each other.

Quintus swung his sword in an arc and Adir ducked quickly to dodge. Quintus twisted his grip on the moving blade and tore it downward. Adir sprawled away and the sword rasped on the flagstone. Quintus' nailed sandals clattered as he ran after Adir. Adir was back on his feet and blocked the blow. They strained against each other, blades locked, and Adir felt his strength paling before Quintus' might. He did not know how long he could hold out. But his mind was relieved of the worry of pondering it. Quintus slammed his fist into Adir's chest, throwing him back and robbing the breath from his lungs.

He staggered away, wary of Quintus' next move. Quintus laughed aloud. He knew he was in control of the fight.

Adir smiled as he felt the strength and rage roaring back into every fiber of his body. He burst forward, howling savagely and slashed at Quintus. Quintus brought his own sword up to block, while rotating it away from him. But the swords never met. Adir pulled his back, reversing it in his grip, and ducked under Quintus' blade. He stabbed back as he lunged past his opponent, still rushing past with every bit of his first momentum. The tip ran true, hissing through the air for Quintus' leg, where his battle gear did not protect it. Quintus twisted away from the thrust, but the tip still cut deep and ripped at his leg.

Adir jumped away, clear of Quintus, and smiled with satisfaction.

"First blood."

Quintus' jaw set and his expression hardened like tempered steel. Adir knew that the wound should have caused a great deal of pain and was unsettled by the cool lethality of his foe's countenance. Quintus thrust suddenly. Adir whirled to defend himself, but could not parry the blade. And yet, the deadly tip stopped short and Quintus withdrew it with a rigid smile on his lips. Adir knew he was probing, exploring the limits of his foe, and playing him. Adir was all too suddenly, and far too late, aware that Quintus was far better than him, and he would have to bend to his will to survive the fight.

Abruptly, Quintus' sword hammered down, like the tool of a smith working an anvil. Adir blocked, but the devastating force nearly ended him. His grip weakened and his blade was tossed aside like chaff. Adir sidestepped as the blow fell, but his arm ached significantly and his nerves rang with the force of the impact. His stomach knotted at the thought of Quintus' power. He was just enduring the least of it, and that terrified him.

Quintus cut down again and Adir blocked instinctively, but the blow never landed. Quintus instead pulled his sword away and seized the wrist of Adir's sword arm. Adir winced as the arm was jerked down, causing him to bend awkwardly. He tried to throw up his other arm, but Quintus batted it away as if nothing. He wrenched the young man's wrist in his grip. A sharp cry of pain escaped Adir's lips and his sword fell from his grasp. A grin dancing on the corners of his lips, Quintus forced Adir back, leaning precariously on his heels.

Then the Roman swung down his arm and crashed the pommel of his gladius into his foe's face. Blood splattered and flowed freely from his nose and mouth. Adir's breathing was quick and ragged. Again, Quintus blasted the pommel of his sword into his face. Then he stomped on the youth's ankle, with painful cries on the part of the latter, and swung him onto the ground, hard. He lowered his blade and let the cold tip rest on the soft flesh of his throat just below the chin. Scarlet blood was pouring down his face and neck.

"You said that if I let the people live, I would have your life. Well, now I have you. So I think they'll die, too."

CHAPTER SEVENTEEN

"Get all the Christians!" Quintus shouted. "Put them in chains."

Adir was scarcely aware of what they were doing. Quintus heaved him onto his feet and slapped manacles around his wrists. He was shoved into place along a line with the others.

The whole ordeal was grimly familiar to him. Titus was shoved into line as well, clearly barely retaining his consciousness, but protesting loudly nonetheless. "I'm not a Christian. I'm not. Please, I'm not part of this. Please, don't..." He was cut off as Quintus struck him across the face.

"Valerius should have killed you the second you tried to desert."

Quintus took his place leading the line of captives, as he had months before when he led Adir and the others through the streets of Rome.

"Where are we going?" Adir asked shakily.

"Decimus is in the city and he's having a party on the outskirts of the city in his villa. You will be the lighting through the night."

Adir hung his head in disbelief. So they were going to be burned to death. And Titus, denying the faith. With considerable effort on his part, he cleared his mind and focused on the task of walking. One step, another.

It was well after dark when Quintus stopped them. They were in the villa courtyard, and all around them the sounds of revelry and celebration echoed from the building.

Quintus, Valerius, and the dozen Praetorians who accompanied them began to unshackle each Christian. Afterward, Quintus lifted his torch until the wavering orange light shown on the sky twenty feet up. Poles lined one side of the courtyard. And, at their top, two stories off the ground, a length of chain connected them. At intervals of two or three yards, another chain connected to this and ran down to the ground where it joined large cylindrical cages, big enough for a man each.

Adir's stomach was in knots. A few of the Praetorians appeared with buckets, and went down the line, thoroughly drenching each captive in the contents. Adir saw that they kept their torches well away from it, and he knew that it had to be oil, flammable oil. And he was soaked in it. He saw that they splashed the cages as well.

A moment later they took up their swords and began to prod the captives toward the terrible metal structures, with harsh commands of, "In the cages, now!"

Adir stood where he was until Quintus slapped the flat of his blade into his back and he reluctantly crawled into the cage. The metal was jagged and painful. Quintus shut the bottom of the cage and latched it securely. Adir shut his eyes and began to pray. He begged God and Christ for anything, anything at all, even a quick death, if that was the only way to be saved. Then came a thought, a flash of hope. Diomed was still out there. So far as he knew, he had not been captured. Perhaps he had been killed, but Adir needed to hope, and he hoped and prayed with all of his might that somehow, Diomed could still help. The only alternative was to burn to death in a giant bird cage dangling twenty feet from the ground.

The cages were hoisted up by way of their connecting chains and they began to rise, dragging themselves off of the ground and ascending slowly. They swayed perilously as they gained height until at last they were at their highest altitude.

Titus was in the cage directly adjacent Adir's, and the latter stared distantly at his fellow, not knowing quite what to think.

As he looked, a blur flashed through his line of vision and lodged itself in one of the links in the chain right next to Titus' cage. Titus reached through the bars and snapped off the shaft of the arrow. A note was attached. Unravelling it, he saw that it read, *Diomed. Escape. Go to Red Sea.*

Titus looked up to Adir and read it aloud. Titus reached up and took hold of the arrowhead, trying

THE VICTOR PART II

to work through the chain where it was lodged, prying it apart. Adir looked away from where Titus labored tediously and saw Quintus take a torch and light one end of the chains, soaked in the flammable oil like everything else.

The flame flickered up the chain and spread down its length. As it passed each cage, it set it alight. Adir began to hear cries of agony. He saw bright flares as the captives burned, and he was absolutely terrified. As it passed his cage, the bars all around him began to blaze almost instantly. He shrank away from the fire but in only a second or so his tunic caught alight. Titus grunted as the fire reached his cage and the searing heat sprang to life around him. With one final, supreme effort he threw all his weight and strength onto the chain and the arrowhead. He heard a definitive *snap!* The chain broke. Titus' cage dropped suddenly, crashing violently into Adir's. Titus plummeted as he dropped, but his terrible scream was cut short when his cage struck the ground, mangling the metal and ringing through the courtyard.

Adir was tossed back inside his cage and suddenly the bottom fell out. The latch had been shattered in the collision with the other cage. He dropped precipitously but caught himself on the bottom bar of his cage. He dangled precariously for a moment, and then the main chain broke entirely. All the cages dropped and Adir was flung into

237

emptiness. The world rushed and spun around him. Then, he landed. The force racked his body and his breath was ripped away. He reeled as his flaming cage crashed into the ground only feet from him. He rolled and stood, immediately sprinting away.

"After him!" Quintus shouted.

Ever in his mind as he ran rang that horrible shriek as Titus had fallen, and the instant it disappeared, as he hit the ground. His whole world once again tumbling down around him, he ran on, until the blackness of night surrounded him.

TO BE CONTINUED AND CONCLUDED IN THE VICTOR PART III

ABOUT THE AUTHOR

Andrew Meade is the young author of *The Victor Part I*.
He is currently occupying his time with school and writing
The Victor Part III, along with other works. He lives in
western Kentucky.

Cover art is an original sketch by Andrew Meade.